Summer on the Run

Nancy Belgue

Orca Book Publishers

National Library of Canada Cataloguing in Publication Data

Belgue, Nancy, 1951-
Summer on the run / Nancy Belgue.

ISBN 1-55143-372-9

I. Title.

PS8553.E4427S86 2005 jC813'.6 C2005-900691-9

Library of Congress Control Number: 2005921066

Summary: During the Depression, Douglas is wanted by the police. His sister Doris tries desperately to protect him until the two hear that their father has been spotted in a nearby town and they head off on an adventure together.

Orca Book Publishers gratefully acknowledges the support for its publishing programs provided by the following agencies: the Government of Canada through the Book Publishing Industry Development Program (BPIDP), the Canada Council for the Arts, and the British Columbia Arts Council.

Cover design: Lynn O'Rourke
Typesetting: John van der Woude
Cover Artwork: James Bentley

Orca Book Publishers
Box 5626 Station B
Victoria, BC Canada
V8R 6S4

Orca Book Publishers
PO Box 468
Custer, WA USA
98240-0468

Printed and bound in Canada
08 07 06 05 • 5 4 3 2 1

To the memory of the real Doris and Douglas
and to brothers and sisters everywhere!

Chapter 1

"Fight! Fight!"

A crowd had gathered in the back of the schoolyard. Dirt scuffed into the air, creating the feeling of a dust bowl.

"Hit 'em, Spiffy!" the grade eight boys yelled.

Doris Stanley craned her neck to see what all the commotion was about. She was sitting underneath the black walnut tree at the edge of the cinder-covered schoolyard. It was June 30, the last day of school before summer vacation, and she was counting the seconds until the bell rang and she was free of classrooms and textbooks for two whole months.

"Your brother's in a fight, Doris!" yelled Johnnie Mullins, their next-door neighbor. "He's whuppin' Spiffy Spafford for calling your dad a lousy hobo."

Doris ran for the shouting crowd of children. If Douglas got caught fighting again, he'd be expelled and lose his chance to go to high school. If that happened, he'd never be able to go to college no matter how smart he was. Darn his bad temper, anyway. Mother was always telling him to get a hold of himself, that his temper was going to be his undoing.

As she got closer to the melee, she heard grunting, along with the meaty sound of fists hitting flesh. She pushed her way through the tightly knit throng of boys and girls. Douglas was in the middle of the choking cloud of dust, and three bigger boys were circling him. He had a cut under one eye and a bloody nose. His good shirt was torn and bloodstained. He looked mad, all right, but behind his eyes, Doris could see he was worried. Three against one were odds not even Douglas could handle.

"Your old man's probably begging for relief right now. I heard my Uncle John telling Sloanie that he ain't even got the nerve to ride the rails."

Douglas raised his fists the way Doris had seen Father show him. He was a terrific boxer, and most of the boys knew it. They kept their distance unless there were at least three of them.

"Cowards," yelled Doris. "You leave my brother alone."

"Hey, Stanley, looks like your baby sister's here

to protect you," Spiffy Spafford sneered as he shuffled toward Douglas, waving his fists.

"Yeah, Stanley. Guess you'll be all right now. Run home and get your momma so she can fight your battles for you too," called Ronnie Mitchell.

"Get out of here, Doris," Douglas said over his raised fists. "Get out of here before you get hurt."

"No." Doris planted her feet beside her brother's. "I'm not going anywhere." She raised her fists the way Douglas was holding his.

A girl in the crowd tittered. Doris didn't give a darn. She wasn't one of them, with their muslin dresses and hair bows. She had no time for all those girls with their silly gossip and tea parties. They never invited her over to their houses anyway, and they said she was a strange girl, always wanting to wear trousers and tag along with her brother's friends. Let them snicker like a bunch of cackling hens. She was a Stanley. And being a Stanley stood for something. They fought their own battles, and all the stuck-up goody-goodies in school could go whistle Dixie for all she cared.

Spiffy was circling Douglas now, crouched low, darting his head back and forth, his chin jutting out aggressively.

"Your old man's nothin' but a bum," Spiffy jeered as he jabbed his fists at Douglas' head.

Douglas wasn't speaking; he was too busy watching Spiffy's fists. He danced backward every time the other boy threw a punch. "Get back, Doris," he said again. "You're just making things worse."

Doris stepped aside, but she kept her eye on Spiffy's friends. Ronnie and Mick had moved to one side, confident that Spiffy was moving in for the kill. One on one was a fair fight, and Doris aimed to keep it that way. She picked up a rock.

Spiffy kept throwing punches that connected with nothing but air. Douglas bobbed and weaved, moving his head so fast it looked like a ball on the end of a bolo bat.

Mavis Miller clutched her hands under her chin and batted her eyelashes. "I think your brother is just the bravest boy," she whispered to Doris.

Doris couldn't take her eyes off Spiffy. He was tiring and his punches were coming less often and with less force. He was getting frustrated, and it was making him meaner. She didn't have time for lovesick girls. Girls had always liked Douglas. The only time any of them ever talked to her was when they were trying to get her to put in a good word with her brother. Mavis Miller was better than most. Doris even kind of liked her.

"Duck, Douglas!" Doris yelled when she saw Mick Malone coming around behind.

It was too late. Mick jumped on Douglas' back and held on. Before Doris could launch her rock, Spiffy landed an uppercut to Douglas' jaw. Doris saw his head snap back.

"Ohhhhh!" the crowd gasped.

"You lousy cowards," Doris yelped as she jumped into the clouds of dust.

"Get away, Doris," grunted Douglas as he spun around, trying to dislodge Mick from his back.

Doris picked up a branch of a tree and clubbed the back of Mick's head.

"You're going to kill him, Doris," cried Mavis. "Someone get a teacher!"

Mick Malone dropped to the dust with a howl, holding his head in his hands. Douglas rounded on Doris.

"Remind me to beat the stuffin' out of you later."

"You're welcome," Doris said with a grin.

Douglas grinned back, then turned, looking for Spiffy. Spiffy was clawing at the crowd, trying to find a way out.

"Why don't you finish what you started?" yelled Doris at his retreating back.

"You Stanleys!" shouted Mr. Ronson as he waded through the throng. "Get over here."

Mr. Ronson was over six feet tall and strong as a bear. Doris had heard Phil LaCasse say he never knew what getting the strap was all about until he got it from Mr. Ronson.

"To the office." He pointed at the school. "You too, Doris."

"She didn't have anything to do with it," Douglas said.

"Well, I hear differently. This is the third time this month." He grabbed Douglas' collar as he went by, and Doris wanted to kick him in the shins.

"Miss Philips, send someone for their mother," Mr. Ronson ordered as he marched the two of them into the office.

He left them sitting on a hard wooden bench in the hall in view of everyone. Doris kept her chin up high, even when Rosie and Louise strolled by on their way to their last class of the day. Douglas' nose had swollen and his eye was practically closed. The bell rang and voices rose in happy chatter. It was the last period of the last day of school, June 1931.

Doris watched as Spiffy Spafford and Mick Malone walked out scot-free. She blinked back a tear. Stanleys don't cry, she told herself. Douglas kept clearing his throat because the blood was dripping down his nostrils. Mavis came by and handed Douglas a handkerchief. He smiled, even though his lips were swollen. In fact, Doris thought, his whole face looked like a Halloween pumpkin that had been smashed on the road.

"What are you going to do this summer, Douglas?" Mavis asked brightly. As if she couldn't see the serious trouble he was in. Girls! thought Doris. Heaven help me.

To her great surprise, Douglas blushed a little and said, "Don't know. Try and get some work, probably."

"Perhaps you could come over one evening," Mavis said. She shifted her books from one arm to another. Her bobbed hair shone in the dusty light from the hall window.

"And wouldn't your father just love that?" mut-tered Doris under her breath. Mavis' father owned the dairy and had a mighty fine opinion of himself.

"Maybe," Douglas said from between his swol-len lips.

Doris gave Douglas a quick glance. What was he saying? Maybe! Mavis Miller? She looked at her brother as if she'd never seen him before.

He shoved her with his shoulder. "Close that mouth of yours before a bee flies in," he said.

"Mavis Miller?"

Douglas crossed his arms and grunted. It was obvious he'd seen the error of his ways, thought

Doris. It was lucky she'd been here. Who knows what might have happened? She was so busy thinking about the strange things that go on when you least expect them that she didn't even notice her mother coming down the hallway until she swept past them and into the principal's office. Douglas stood up as if to say something, but his mother's expression stopped him dead in his tracks. She held out her hand as if to say, "Stop. I don't want to hear it," and shut the door behind her.

Doris could hear the voices of Mr. Ronson and her mother rising and falling. She strained to make out what they were saying, but could catch only the occasional word.

"third time..."

"no choice..."

"sorry..."

"any word?"

"expel..."

Doris leaned her head on Douglas' shoulder. She could tell by the way he was sitting, still and hard as a piece of wood, that he could hear the same words.

The school was empty and quiet by the time her mother and Mr. Ronson opened the door.

"Well, Douglas," said Mr. Ronson, "your mother has persuaded me to overlook this incident today because my sources inform me that you were not the instigator of this particular altercation." He paused and smiled in Mother's direction. Doris felt like gagging.

"What do you say, Douglas?" asked Mother.

Mr. Ronson leaned forward. "Yes, son? I can't hear you."

"Douglas," said Mother. Her voice sounded tired. Doris looked at her carefully. She looked worried, too. And older. Doris glanced at Douglas. His head was down and his hands were clenched into fists. Douglas always found it difficult to apologize. "Do it, Doug," Doris whispered. "Do it for Mother."

"I'm sorry for fighting, sir," Douglas said in a voice almost too small to hear.

"What's that?"

"He said he's sorry," Doris shouted.

"Doris!" said Mother.

"Well, I'm sorry I yelled," Doris said. "But Douglas didn't start it. And it was three to one, and Spiffy Spafford called Father a drunken bum, and all Douglas did was tell him to take a hike because his father was a lying cheat—"

"That's enough, Doris!" Mother's voice was shaking.

Mr. Ronson leaned toward her and said, "Can I get you a glass of water."

Mother shook her head. "No, thank you. That's very kind. But if you don't mind, I think we'd better get going."

Mr. Ronson gave Mother a stern look and handed her a piece of paper. "This is my home address. I want you to let me know how Douglas gets along this summer. I want to know if he stays out of trouble. I'll decide whether or not I'll recommend he begin high school based on what he does during the next two months."

Mother took the paper reluctantly and looked at it as if it were a death sentence.

"Hear that, young man?"

Douglas' face had turned deep red. Doris squeezed his hand and shut her eyes. Don't say anything, Doug, she prayed. Just nod.

"Yes, sir."

Doris opened her eyes, surprised. Had he read her mind? But he was staring straight ahead. Beside them, Mother slumped visibly.

"All right then. You may go."

Mother put the sheet of paper in her handbag. "Doris, Douglas." She nodded at Mr. Ronson and started down the hall.

Douglas snapped his hand out of Doris's. He marched down the hall behind Mother.

Doris went last. Douglas was limping a little, but trying not to show it. Just like always.

Mother had pulled her shoulders back and drawn her chin up. She looked like a queen on the way to her coronation. Doris followed behind, wishing, as usual, that she could make everything better.

Chapter 2

It sure didn't feel like the first day of summer vacation. Mother had gone off to her job, cleaning houses in Walkerville. Doug had disappeared right after breakfast without saying where he was going or when he'd be back. What if he tried to pick another fight with Spiffy? Doris chewed on the edge of her thumb and remembered what Mr. Ronson had told Douglas about staying out of trouble. Doug was smart. He wouldn't mess up his chance to finish high school. Mother wanted him to be the first Stanley to go to college. She wasn't giving up on that dream, even if life was different now.

And ever since Father had disappeared, life sure hadn't been the same. Hard times made hard men, said the junk man who came up and down the streets, hauling away the trash other families couldn't get any more use out of. Mother never talked about Father; neither did the neighbors, but Doris knew he'd left them. Just taken off to ride the rails, leaving Mother to try to keep things together.

Some people can't deal with pressure, said Mrs. Murphy, who lived up the block. She was talking about the rich folks in Detroit who'd jumped out of their windows when they lost all their money in the stock market crash two years ago. Doris couldn't figure out why people would kill themselves over money. There were a lot worse things to lose. Like a father.

Doris sat on her front porch and watched her street come to life. Across the way lived the Grants. In past summers, Doris had played with Lila, but this year Lila was going to stay with her aunt and uncle on their farm in Delhi. Her family wanted her to work, picking tobacco and minding her cousins. Hank Vanderhaven and his family had moved two months ago and their house stood empty. Couldn't pay the rent no more, Mr. Vanderhaven had told Mother on the day they moved away. Doris didn't know where they'd gone.

She hauled out her old dictionary and looked up her word for the day. The kids all called her WAD (word-a-day) girl because she had a new word every day and used it. It was part of her plan to get better.

Not even this dumb old Depression was going to stop her improving herself.

It sure was hot. Doris flipped through the *Funk & Wagnall's* she'd lifted out of a junk heap outside one of the Walkerville mansions. Hotter 'n blazes and not yet ten o'clock. The radio said it was going to be a record breaker. She fanned herself with an old piece of the *Border City Star* that Mother brought home from her job. They always got the news one day late, but at least they got the news, which was more than most families on her street. And she got to read the funny papers. Her favorite was "Little Orphan Annie." The scent of the lilac bush that grew beside the porch made her smile. How bad could life be with lilacs to smell, a porch to sit on, the funny papers to read and a whole summer vacation ahead of her?

She scanned the dictionary and picked out *inferno*. That's what today was like, an inferno. The dictionary said *inferno* meant *hell*. She was just contemplating how she could use that word without getting Mother's dander up, when Barbara Mullins scuffed out onto her porch in bare feet. All the kids on Rices Road went barefoot in the summer. No one had money for shoes these days.

"Hey, Doris," Barbara yelled when she saw her. "Want to go swimming?"

"Sure," Doris called back. "It's an inferno out there today."

Barbara rolled her eyes. Doris smirked.

The beach was already crowded with folks trying to cool down. Doris and Barbara found a piece of sand near the pier, dropped their shorts and splashed across the slippery, slimy bottom of the Detroit River. The cold water rippled over her skin, making Doris numb to the bone. Overhead the seagulls dipped and screeched, wheeling through the sky like flashes of summer clouds. All around her, voices rose in excited shrieks as boys and girls pushed each other off the pier and into the water.

Barbara and Doris took turns standing upside down on their hands, while clouds of river bottom sand rose up around their faces and got into their noses. Every so often a boat, way out on the river, sounded its horn.

Summer was well and truly underway.

"I'm starving," Barbara said once they were out of the water and sunning themselves on the sand.

"Me too," said Doris, listening to the growl of her stomach instead of the happy shrieks of the bathers.

"I wish we'd brought some food."

"Well, we didn't." Doris slapped her stomach like she meant business. Enough of this silly growling.

She didn't want to tell Barbara that there hadn't been any food to bring. Her stomach sounded an alarm, gurgling like water in a stopped-up drain.

"Hey, Barbara! Hey, Doris!" called a voice behind them.

Doris and Barbara turned their heads just in time to see Barbara's big brother, Johnnie, walking toward them on his hands.

"Look at me!" he shouted.

A crowd of little kids followed him as he made his way down the entire length of the beach. The kids laughed and clapped, and when Johnnie flipped himself to his feet and took a bow, one of the mothers even gave him a dime.

"Johnnie, share with us," Barbara pleaded when she saw the dime.

"Sure," Johnnie said with a grin. "That's thirty cents I made already today. I started at Ford Beach and made twenty cents there." Doris gave Johnnie a sideways look. He had grown over the winter and gotten muscles. Doris blushed.

Doris, Barbara and Johnnie gathered their clothes together and headed toward home. At Ferguson's store, they stopped for ice cream. Johnnie paid fifteen cents for three cones, and they sat on the curb eating them.

Doris' stomach growled its gratitude. The sun

slanted through the trees: Doris closed her eyes and listened to the sounds of summer. Somewhere off to the right, a screen door slapped shut, and Doris could hear the creak of a clothesline as someone hung out laundry to dry. The clopping sound of a horse's hooves and a clanging bell told her that the knife sharpener was coming down the block. In the distance she could still hear the sounds of the screaming and yelling of the bathers.

She took another slurp of her maple walnut ice cream and let herself think of all the great times that lay ahead of her that summer. She wouldn't let Father's being gone spoil it for her. Nor was she going to lie awake at night anymore, listening for Mother's quiet crying. She wasn't going to watch Doug like a mother hen, either. He was thirteen and he knew enough to stay out of trouble.

She sighed and let the rich mapley cream trickle down her throat. Treats should last forever, she decided, trying to catch a drop of melting heaven before it fell onto the dusty ground between her bare feet. But then they wouldn't be treats, her practical brain told her. But then every day sure would be special, she countered, trying to decide which she would really like better.

Johnnie took a thoughtful slurp of his ice cream and said, "Where's Douglas today?"

Doris opened her eyes. There was something about the way he'd said that. Too casual, as if he knew something she didn't.

"What do you mean, Johnnie Mullins?" she asked, not noticing the drip of maple cream that was about to escape her tongue.

"Nothin'."

"That's not so. You asked me funny."

Johnnie took a bite of his cone and chewed slowly. "Hear he's gotten himself in with a bad lot."

Johnnie wasn't acting funny now. His eyes were serious.

"What do you mean?" The ice cream was dripping hard now, like a leaky faucet. Doris didn't care. She wasn't hungry for ice cream anymore.

"Buddy Hayes saw him down at the river last night. With Pierre LaPierre."

"He wouldn't do that." Doris' heart started thumping.

"I hope Buddy's wrong, Doris, but I don't know. Douglas told me he was going to try and get some money."

"He didn't mean rumrunning."

Johnnie put one foot on the curb and rested his elbow on his knee. Doris tossed the rest of her cone into the garbage. "I hope not, Doris," Johnnie said, looking down at her. "It's getting dangerous out there now. The crash has made the gangs real desperate. There's been lots of shootings over in Detroit. I read about it in the *Star* just the other day. It's not like it used to be. He'd be best to stay away."

"He isn't doing anything like that, Johnnie Mullins, and don't you say he is," Doris said.

Johnnie Mullins gave Doris one of his I-know-more-than-you-do-'cause-you're-just-a-kid looks. "Just remember what I said, Doris. He'd be best to stay away." He took his foot off the curb and turned away. "I'm going to try and get a few more cents today. Thought I'd try juggling next." He pulled three balls from his pocket and tossed them one by one into the air as he sauntered back toward the crowds at the beach.

"Forget about Johnnie," Barbara said when he was gone. "He thinks he's so smart."

But Doris couldn't help wondering. Just exactly how was Douglas going to get extra money? Just what was he planning to do?

Barbara put her hand on Doris' shoulder. "Race you," she said.

Doris tried to smile. "All the way home?"

"On your mark, get set, go!" shrieked Barbara and took off at full speed.

"Hey, not fair!" yelled Doris, launching herself off the sidewalk.

Their chests were heaving by the time they got to Rices Road. Doris was laughing so hard she could barely run, but Barbara was laughing even harder, so the two of them collapsed on the corner, next to the graveyard, and stared up into the leaf-laced sky.

"I can't wait for all the stuff we do in the summer," Barbara said dreamily. "Potato roasts at midnight," she began.

"Baseball games against the Pitt Street Pirates," Doris said.

"The first all-day sucker," added Barbara.

"Excursions to Prince Road Park to ride the merry-go-round," said Doris. "And don't forget Saturday afternoon shows at the Tivoli." She closed her eyes and relaxed. Summer spread out in front of her in one long golden ribbon, promising nothing but fun and...she sat up suddenly.

"What's wrong?" Barbara asked, opening her eyes.

"I forgot something," Doris answered, getting to her feet.

"Doris, what is it?" said Barbara, propping herself on one elbow and squinting into the sun.

"Gotta go," Doris said, taking off at a run.

"Doris!" Barbara yelled behind her.

Doris kept running. Her heart pounded as she raced across Howard Avenue and headed for home. Douglas wouldn't dare, she thought, he wouldn't *dare*!

It had come to her in a blinding flash. It must have been thinking about all the summer traditions that did it. She could hear Douglas saying it just last summer while he was fishing in the river. "Sure wouldn't be hard to get from here to Michigan." He was standing on the dock, looking out toward Belle Isle.

"Why'd you want to do that?" Doris had asked.

"Never you mind, Pipsqueak," he'd said.

Then Father had disappeared, and she'd heard Douglas talking to Vinnie Goldman about something. She'd caught them just last week when she was walking home from school and saw them talking by the cemetery gates. Vinnie Goldman was known more for the trouble he got into than anything else. Why, his father had been in business with Al Capone back during the twenties, or so Mrs. Mullins said. Still had rumrunning connections, too, according to Jillson Jones, who worked at one of the roadhouses out on Riverside Drive.

Things were starting to add up, and Doris didn't like what they came to. Maybe Johnnie knew what he was talking about after all. How could she have been so dumb? Doris collapsed, chest heaving, on the front steps of her house. She could just see Mother's face if Douglas got caught rumrunning between Windsor and Detroit. He was only thirteen. He could ruin his whole life.

She stopped to think where he might have gone. She'd heard the stories about rumrunners who had boats that sailed from the export docks, as folks called them, and took loads of whiskey across the river to Detroit. But she didn't know exactly where these docks were. If only Douglas weren't so stubborn. He never thought he was going to fail at anything. Doris wrung her hands and stared nervously down the street. It wasn't even lunchtime yet, and Douglas still had a whole day to get into trouble.

Think! she commanded herself. Where could he have gone? Think!

Barbara arrived panting like an old dog at the bottom of her front walk. "What the heck, Doris Stanley," she demanded, "did you think you were doing?"

"Can't talk now," Doris said. She went inside and let the screen door slap behind her. She couldn't let anyone, not even Barbara see how worried she was. If Douglas really was up to no good, she'd have to find out first. Then she'd figure out what to do next. First things first, as Mother always said.

Thinking of Mother made Doris close her eyes and rub her hands against her face. Mother! She looked so frail these days, as if the weight of the whole world was pressing her into the baking hot street. Doris pounded her scrunched-up fist on the table.

She would find that brother of hers, and she would make him promise not to take any stupid risks!

Doris went out onto the back porch and down toward the little patch of vegetables that Mother and she had planted back in May, right after the danger of frost had passed. They had nasturtiums because Mother said they were full of vitamins. And lettuce, tomatoes and cabbages. It was Doris' job to keep the kitchen garden weeded and watered, and she always did some of her best thinking there among the cabbages. As she squatted amidst the leafy fronds of the baby carrots, she was hit with an idea.

Vinnie kept a boat at the bottom of Pillette Street.

That's where Douglas would go if he was up to no good.

Doris dropped her trowel and took off at a trot toward the river. She had just started off when Douglas and Vinnie came roaring by her, heading in the opposite direction, running so fast their faces seemed pulled back into a grimace. A policeman was following them on foot, and in the distance one of the Windsor police cars followed along behind. Doris' breath caught in her throat. The principal's words came back to her: "I'll decide whether or not I'll recommend he begin high school based on what he does during the next two months." Darn it all, anyway! If she could remember how important his good behavior was, why couldn't he?

"Douglas!" yelled Doris as he sped past. He didn't even glance her way. He and Vinnie disappeared into a laneway that cut behind the playing card factory and ran like blazes for another alleyway. Doris played in those alleys all the time and knew them like a road map. Doug was heading for the cemetery, no doubt about it. The police car roared by, making Doris think of the Keystone Cops. Only this wasn't funny or the movies. This was real life and Douglas, darn him, was heading for very big trouble.

Doris ran after the police car and turned onto Giles Boulevard just in time to see the car turning the other way on Howard Avenue. She screeched to a stop and sauntered as casually as could be in the other direction. The running police officer turned and looked at her suspiciously.

"Hey, little girl," yelled the officer when he saw her. "You see two boys go by here? About thirteen years old?"

Doris froze in her tracks. "No, sir," she said.

The policeman narrowed his eyes. "You sure? They went right by here. Running like the dickens."

"No, sir," Doris said again.

"Why were you running then? Looked to me like you were chasing someone."

"Looking for my dog," Doris said, hoping she wouldn't be struck dead for telling all these lies.

"Hmmm." The officer signaled to the police car that was circling the block. "Well, if you do see anything, you have a duty to report it to the police. You know that, don't you?"

Doris nodded. This must be what sinking into fresh mud felt like.

"All right then. You get on home. And watch out for those two. We've had our eyes on them for a while and they're a dangerous pair. They let the air out of the tires of the police car." He nodded at the police car as it sputtered to a stop at the curbside. "And not only are they in trouble for vandalizing police property, they've been spotted out on the river and the Coast Guard wants us to round them up for questioning. They're in very serious trouble, little girl. You got that?" He glared at her with angry eyes.

Doris shivered. By the time she got back home, her knees were shaking so hard she could barely stand.

Douglas had doubled back through the cemetery and was sitting in the kitchen, his face white as chalk.

"Douglas Stanley, you are a wanted man," Doris said as she filled a glass with water and drank deeply.

"Don't tell Mother," Douglas said.

"What are you and Vinnie going to do? Hide from the police all summer?"

"No," Douglas said in a low voice.

"You can't risk everything that Mother hopes for and break the law, Douglas. That's not going to help anything."

Douglas stood up and started to pace around the kitchen. "We hardly have enough food to eat." He gestured angrily at the empty breadbox. "When was the last time we had any bread? Or meat? We can't live on popcorn and beans for the rest of the summer. Someone's got to do something!"

"At least we have *something* to eat, Doug. There's others who aren't so lucky."

"Stop trying to sound all brave and good like Mother," Doug snapped. "There's money to be made on that river, and I'm going to make it."

"No, Doug!" Doris said. "Johnnie Mullins says it's way more dangerous than it used to be. I read something in the *Star* just last week about the Purple Gang in Detroit and how they've been shooting anyone who tries to move in on their rumrunning business."

"No one's going to shoot us up, Doris. We're just a couple of kids. But if I can make two dollars for every case of whiskey I get across that river, then we're going to have enough to eat, and Mother won't have to work day and night like she does now."

Douglas made it all sound so easy that Doris could almost believe him. In fact, for a moment, just a tiny moment, she could almost see herself helping him load the crates and shove the boat into the water, the music of the roadhouse wafting out over the river as they paddled for Michigan.

She snapped out of it, just in time. What was she thinking? If Douglas got caught, his future would be ruined. And Mother would be mortified.

"Douglas, that's just plain crazy talk."

"Say what you want, Doris, but Vinnie and I are making a run tonight."

"You can't!"

"Oh, yes, I can." He leaned forward and stared into Doris' eyes. "And don't you say a word about it, neither."

Doris went back out to finish weeding the garden. Every time she heard a noise, she jumped, thinking it might be the police coming back to look for Douglas. All the fun had gone out of the day, out of summer and out of life. She flopped down on the grass and stared up at the clouds of lilacs that drifted against the summer sky. She could hear her mother saying, Stop being so dramatic, Doris Stanley. Nothing's as bad as you make it out to be.

Well, thought Doris, this is about as bad as it can be. She rolled over on her stomach and started searching for a four-leaf clover. Last summer she'd found one once in this very patch of grass, and the next day she'd won a yo-yo at the Sunday School picnic.

"What are you doing?" asked Barbara.

Doris held up a four-leaf clover. "Found one!"

Barbara plunked herself down. "Where did you go, anyway?"

"Left something on the stove," Doris said, avoiding Barbara's eyes. She was no good at fibbing, her mother said, because she turned bright red whenever she tried to tell a whopper.

"Did not. You're not even allowed to use the stove when your mother's not home."

"Well, maybe I've got a secret, Barbara Mullins."

"Is it about your brother?"

Doris looked up, eyes wide. "How did you know?"

"I just do." Barbara pulled up a blade of grass, held it taut between her thumbs and blew. A loud, jagged-sounding honking noise split the air.

Doris put the four-leaf clover in her pocket. If Barbara knew and Johnnie knew and even Doris knew, lots of others might know as well. If word got back to the police, they'd come looking.

Doris had a feeling that she was going to need all the four-leaf clovers she could find.

Chapter 3

Doris drummed her fingers on the porch rail.

Inside, Mother was ironing. The rhythmic slap and hiss of the iron on the sheets, and the smell of the freshly ironed cloth, usually gave Doris the feeling that all was right with the world. But not tonight. She closed her eyes and tried not to think of the fact that Douglas had gotten up right after supper, given Doris one of his hard stares and told Mother he was going to play some pickup ball over in the vacant lot. That had been six thirty, and he still wasn't back, even though it was almost ten thirty and Mother would be wanting to get to bed soon.

"It's going to be a soggy night," Mother said, her voice carrying through the screen door into the night that buzzed with the sounds of insects.

"Sure is," Doris answered, trying to make her voice sound as normal as possible.

"Where's that brother of yours?"

Doris clenched her jaw. She'd known this was coming and was trying to think how to answer without telling a lie.

Her mother's voice behind her made her jump. "Land sakes, I wish he'd get home." The screen door slapped. Mother had come out on the porch and was peering into the dark. "Lord knows it was dark an hour ago. They can't be playing baseball in the dark." She wiped the back of her neck, picked some damp strands of hair off her face and pushed them back into the bun she wore on the top of her head.

"No, ma'am."

Mother fanned herself with a piece of newspaper. "I can't even hear voices from over that way. Come on, Doris, we're taking a walk."

Mother tugged Doris' hand, and together they started down the hot cement sidewalk toward Giles Boulevard. "He did say he was going to be in the vacant lot at the corner, didn't he?"

"Yes, ma'am."

Her mother stopped and turned to face her. "No, ma'am. Yes, ma'am. Is that all you have to say?"

Doris shook her head. The night was alive with a million insects, and the buzzing seemed to be right inside her head. "No, ma'am."

Mother gave her a questioning look, then hurried her pace a little. They rounded the corner and were headed toward the lot when Doris heard the sound of feet, running.

"Mom, Doris!" It was Douglas, out of breath and soaking wet.

"Where have you been, young man?"

Mother's grip on Doris' hand relaxed just a little.

"We went swimming after the game," Douglas said. "Sorry."

"You know you're not supposed to go swimming in the dark," Mother said. But Doris could hear the smile behind the stern words. Douglas was always sweet-talking Mother into believing what he said.

Doris stared at her brother. He had a hole in the knee of his pants and one in his pocket. He'd been swimming all right. Only it wasn't a swim he'd planned on. She'd bet her bottom dollar on that.

Mother turned and headed toward home, Doris and Douglas following along behind.

"What happened?" Doris whispered, pointing at Doug's ripped trousers.

"Shh!" he said, nodding at Mother's stiff back.

"I'm going to bed," Mother said when they got home. "It's been a long day. Douglas, you close up, please."

Above them, the floorboards creaked as Mother moved around, getting ready for bed.

Douglas pulled Doris out onto the back stoop. "We delivered five cases of whiskey tonight," he said, his eyes shining with excitement. "I made ten dollars."

"Holy cow!" Doris said. "Where is it?"

"See, I told you it was as easy as anything," Douglas said, patting his pockets. His face crumpled. "It's not here!"

"I guess it was until you fell in the water," Doris said, pointing at the hole.

"All that work for nothing." Douglas sat down hard. "I've got about as much luck as Father."

"Did you see Al Capone?" Doris asked, trying to change the subject.

Douglas rolled his eyes. "Al Capone doesn't get involved in penny-ante stuff like a few cases of whiskey. Besides, he's in jail now."

"How would you have explained that money to Mother, anyway?"

The smile faded from Douglas' face. "I hadn't thought of that," he admitted.

"So it's lucky you lost that money after all, Douglas Stanley, because if she ever found out what you're doing, you'd be in so much trouble."

"Hush!" Douglas said. "Did you hear something?"

Doris closed her mouth and listened. She couldn't hear anything but the sound of a thousand million insects.

"No."

Douglas crept to the fence. "I gotta get out of here," he said, shoving past her. He slipped through the hole in the lilac hedge and ran like a streak of gray across the neighboring backyards toward the cemetery gates.

Doris saw it then. The silent police car, its lights doused, cruising to a stop in front of her house. She closed her eyes and said a little prayer. If Doug can only get out of trouble one more time, I promise I'll make him do the right thing. He's a good boy, she telegraphed the dark sky and whoever was up there. He only wanted to help Mother.

She scurried down the path to see where Doug was headed, tripping over the watering can. She was still wiping the dirt off her hands when she heard Mother answering the front door. Doris crept in the back way, tiptoed into the hallway, hid behind the coat rack and listened while her mother invited the policemen into the house. She held her breath while they told Mother that they'd followed a boy from the river where they had seen him rumrunning.

Mother's back looked like a steel spike as she turned and went to the bottom of the stairs. Doris squeezed her eyes tight as she waited. "Douglas," Mother called out. "Come down here."

Douglas wouldn't be coming down the stairs anytime soon. Doris knew she had to do something, had to think of something.

"I'm sorry, officer," said Mother, her voice showing the first sign of worry. "He must be asleep. I'll just go up and get him."

Doris opened her eyes and peeked out from behind the old coats. She could see Mother's feet disappearing up the stairs. In the dimly lit hallway, the two policemen exchanged smug looks.

Think!

Overhead, Mother's footsteps crossed from Douglas' room into the hall and into Doris' room. They picked up speed as she hurried back down the hall and ran down the stairs.

"They're not there," she said, her voice rising in fear. "Neither of them."

"Ma'am?"

"My daughter's gone too." Mother brushed quickly past the policemen and onto the porch. She flicked on the porch light and stared out into the night. "You've got to find them!"

The policemen followed Mother onto the porch. Their voices had changed from accusing to helpful. They could sense Mother's terror. They'd already forgotten they were pursuing a fugitive rumrunner.

"She's only ten years old," Mother said as she started down the walk. The policemen followed her. "My son's just thirteen. Where do you think they could have gone?"

"Don't you worry, ma'am," the bigger, burlier and older policeman said. He patted Mother's arm. Doris crept to the screen door, belly to the floor. Now that the policemen were worried about her, she didn't want them to see her.

The second policeman strode to the police car and turned the key. The engine rumbled to life. This time he switched on the lights, which flooded the dark street. The insect chorus thrummed its disapproval. The car disappeared around the corner.

Doris crawled toward the back of the house, not certain what to do.

"All right, Doris Stanley, you can stop right where you are," Mother said. She was still on the porch, her back to the door. Mothers have two sets of eyes, Doris thought, one in the front and another somewhere in the back of their head.

Without turning around, Mother continued, "Where's your brother?"

Doris rolled over and stared at the tin ceiling. "I don't know."

"Why were you in the garden ten minutes ago?"

Doris sat up and stared at Mother's rigid back.

A thousand moths were circling around her head, making her look like a spooky angel.

"Weeding?" she said.

"As soon as I'm sure the coast is clear, I'm coming in there, and you and I are going to have a straight talk," Mother said out of the side of her mouth as she continued to search the street with her eyes. The police car circled the block and slowed in front of the house.

"Nothing yet, ma'am," said the older policeman. "Try not to worry. I'm sure she's just up to mischief."

"I'm sure you're right," Mother said. "I just wish I knew what."

"Try and get some sleep, ma'am. We'll keep looking."

Mother waved at the officers. They drove off. Douglas had been forgotten.

Mother watched the car until it disappeared around the corner for the second time. Then she turned and came into the house. She sat on the bottom step without turning on a single light.

"Tell me everything, Doris," she said. "And don't tell one fib."

"Douglas and Vinnie Goldman have been rum-running," Doris said, letting out a long, wavery breath. It was good to say it, even if Mother did close her eyes and slump back against the newel post.

"For how long?"

"Just started."

"Where is he?"

"He ran off when he saw the police car. I think he's hiding in the cemetery."

Even though it was dark, Doris could feel her mother looking right into her head where the fibs were stored. "Find him and tell him not to come home tonight. I've got to think of something."

Doris nodded.

"Go out the back door and through the hole in the fence. Cut through the Mullinses' yard, and be careful! I don't want anyone to see you."

Mother stood, walked back to the door and peered out into the moth-flecked darkness. "If you're not back in an hour, I'm going to come looking for you, so don't dawdle."

Doris crossed the hallway and hugged Mother from behind. Some of the stiffness left her spine, and her hands clutched at the arms that circled her waist. "And be careful," she whispered.

Doris nodded against her back, feeling the thinness of her mother's old bathrobe. She went out the back door, inhaling the spicy smell. It was dark, but the moon was high and bright. She crawled through the hole in the Mullinses' fence, just as Mother had said. The dew squelched between her toes as she crossed the yard and then the street to climb the spiky, wrought iron fence that surrounded the graveyard. The graveyard covered an entire city block. It was patrolled by Old Man Barzelli and his rottweiler dog, Killer.

Moonlight bathed Doris as she hoisted one leg over the fence; then the moon sailed behind a bank of spooky-looking clouds. She grazed her thigh when she pulled her left leg over the spike and winced at the warm trickle of blood that ran down her leg. Doris dropped to the ground, crouched in the long grass that bordered the fence, held her breath and listened. Silence. Mr. Barzelli and Killer must be at the other end of the cemetery. Doris had to find Douglas before their rounds brought them back. But where should she start?

There was an old crypt on the west side of the cemetery, near Giles Boulevard. Sometimes Douglas and Johnnie went there to shoot dice. Doris took off at a trot, thankful that the moon had reappeared. The ancient gravestones were silvery in the moonlight, their inscriptions faded to nothing. Dead flowers tipped against the new headstone of a nine-year-old boy who had been buried just last week, the grave still soft and springy underfoot. His mother had fished him out of the river when he hadn't come in from swimming. Doris had seen the funeral on her way home from school. Billy McKenzie had been one of the best swimmers in the neighborhood. His mother had cried, leaning on the arm of Billy's father. Billy's sister, Edith McKenzie, was in Doris' class at school. She'd missed the last week of classes, and now her mother wouldn't let her go to the beach.

Doris jumped when the sky darkened again. She stood still and held her breath. She was sure she'd heard a noise. She looked at Billy's grave, half expecting to see him standing there throwing a baseball into his mitt, just the way he always had.

"Doris!" hissed a voice behind Billy's headstone.

She froze.

"Doris! Did you see Old Man Barzelli?"

A wraithlike arm beckoned to her from the fresh mound of dirt.

"Douglas," Doris hissed back into the darkness as she walked closer to the grave, her heart thundering in her chest. "Mother wants you to stay hidden tonight. The police have been to the house."

"Get down!" Douglas reached up and yanked her into the dirt.

Doris was sure she could hear Billy McKenzie laughing. She brushed the damp earth from her chin.

"Barzelli and Killer were by here fifteen minutes ago. They should be coming back this way any second." Douglas' arm was shaking where he had draped it over her back.

Doris tried to lift her head, but Douglas had her pinned.

"You can't stay here," she whispered. "Killer will smell you, even if Mr. Barzelli doesn't see you."

"Is the coast clear with the cops?"

"They're gone for now. But Mother says you've got to stay hidden tonight. They may be back."

"Shhhh!"

The summer night settled in around them like a damp blanket. Lightning bugs flickered in the trees.

"Hear that?" Douglas lifted his head, sniffing the air like a hunting dog.

"No," Doris said, trying again to lift her head. "Get your arm off my back!"

Douglas was on all fours now, peeking above the mound of dirt. Doris pushed herself up. Then she heard it.

Barking. And cursing.

It was Killer and Mr. Barzelli. She could just make out their shapes among the statues of angels.

They were running.

Right at Billy McKenzie's grave.

Chapter 4

"Run!" Douglas yelled, scrambling to his feet and tugging Doris to hers.

They headed for the fence, zigzagging through the gravestones, hurtling over small statues.

"Stop!" Mr. Barzelli yelled behind them. "You are trespassing. I call the police. You devils!"

Killer's barking got closer and closer.

"Separate!" panted Douglas. "The dog can't follow both of us. You go that way!" He pointed toward the chestnut tree that grew beside the front gate. "You can climb the tree and get over the fence by crawling out the big branch."

"What about you?"

"I'll try and distract them. Go!" He gave her a push and ran the other way.

Doris wanted to go after him, but Killer was already on his scent. Doris sprinted the few remaining feet and hauled herself into the lowest branches of the tree. Mr. Barzelli stopped ten feet from where she huddled, her lungs screaming as she tried to breathe quietly.

Killer's barking faded into the distance, and Doris closed her eyes and swore she would take care of things from now on. If Douglas escaped, she would make sure he stayed out of trouble for the rest of the summer. She would see to it that he got into college, she would glue herself to his heels like his shadow until he was safely back in school. Please let him outrun Killer, she whispered. Please, please, please.

A twig snapped under the tree. She sucked in her breath and froze.

Mr. Barzelli poked the leaves with a long stick. It grazed her ankle. Doris bit her lip. "Rotten keeds," she heard him mutter. "Like devils, running through these graves."

Stab. The stick ruffled the leaves next to her hand.

Stab. A decapitated cone-shaped cluster of flowers fluttered to the ground.

"Keeller!" Mr. Barzelli threw the stick to the ground and strode off in the direction of the dog's frantic barking. "Haf you got one of these devils? Good dog! I come."

Doris let out a long, wavery breath. If only she could see through the leaves and the darkness. Killer's barking was excited and high pitched. She inched along the branch and dropped like a cat onto the pavement. Then she ran as if the ghost of Billy McKenzie were chasing her.

Around the block, onto Howard and toward the other entrance to the cemetery, Doris ran like the wind. There was no sign of Douglas anywhere; the streets were deserted. She flattened herself against the side of the post office and listened. All was quiet. Had Killer eaten Douglas?

Then she heard it. Softly at first, like falling rain, then louder. The sound of running feet. She whirled around and caught a glimpse of a boy disappearing through the alley toward the river.

Douglas.

The cemetery gate clanged. Startled, she swung around and stared. Mr. Barzelli was standing in the entryway, holding Killer by his chain, looking right at her. He took one step onto the pavement.

"Leetle girl. I see you there. I know where you leef! I send police after you." He shook his fist, and Killer growled low in his throat.

Doris turned and ran. He couldn't know who she was. Could he? She didn't stop running until she could smell the river, dank and fishy. Across the water, the lights of Detroit lit up the skyline. Doris sucked some of the cooler air into her burning lungs and collapsed.

When her breath steadied, she patrolled the riverbank, looking for Douglas, but he had disappeared into the night. A far-off clock struck twelve times. Midnight.

Two hours had passed since she'd left the house. Mother would be crazy with worry. Doris knew it was time to go home. Never had she been out so late, alone in the dark streets. She trotted toward home, keeping a steady pace, fear clutching at her stomach with each noise she heard in the shadows.

Here! Cats howling on the porch of an abandoned wooden house.

There! Loud voices raised in anger, smashing glass.

Now! A pair of red eyes peering at her from atop a trash can.

The night was alive with danger. Doris ran.

Mother was on the porch, pacing. She ran down the walk as Doris turned the corner.

"Where have you been?" Mother's arms shook as she hugged Doris to her.

"I found him in the cemetery, but Killer chased us and he ran one way, I went another. I climbed the tree and got away, then I saw him running through the back alley toward the river. I followed him, but I couldn't find him." The pounding of Mother's heart drowned out Doris' words. She looked up. Mother was searching the street with her eyes.

"I've made a decision," Mother said. She held Doris at arm's length for a moment. Then she pulled Doris into the house and sat her at the kitchen table.

"Decision?" Doris asked, watching Mother as she spooned some tea into an old chipped pot.

"We're moving."

Moving! How would Douglas find them?

"Tomorrow, I want you to find your brother. Tell him to meet us at the train station on Saturday morning. We're going to spend the summer on Point Pelee."

"What?" Doris' head was spinning. How could they just up and move? What would happen to their furniture? Their house? How would Father know where they were?

"Mr. Mullins saw the police car. He came over after you left." Mother put a mug of tea in front of Doris. It was heavily sweetened, rare these days. Mother must have been worried. The tea tasted like ambrosia would taste, thought Doris, using yesterday's word. She took a greedy sip and watched Mother drum her fingers on the table.

"He said that Douglas is heading for serious trouble. The police are really cracking down on bootleggers, even small fry like your brother." She took a calming sip of tea. "He could go to jail, and now they know where he lives." Doris nodded. The shadows in the kitchen gyrated as a slight breeze sent the old lilac tree outside the window to dancing.

"And I lost my job today." Mother's voice was small.

Doris looked up. Mother was wiping her cheek.

"Mr. Mullins has a brother who needs a place to live for the next few months. He told me that some families pack up and move to the Point during the summer to save rent money. His brother can live here and pay the rent. And I can get Douglas out of Windsor."

"But what about all the summer rituals?" Doris began.

"Shhh," said Mother. "Do you hear something?"

Doris ran to the front door. The police car was back.

"I'll handle this," said Mother, coming up behind her.

"I see the little girl's home safe and sound," said the older officer.

"She just got back."

"Where did you get to, little girl?" asked the other officer.

"She was at a potato roast over on Ottawa Street," Mother said, nudging Doris. "Only she thought she could sneak out without getting caught."

"That right?" asked the first officer.

Doris nodded, unable to speak. Her voice was no more than a squeak.

"She won't be going anywhere anytime soon," said Mother.

The older officer had edged into the hallway and was looking into the dining room. "No sign of your son, then, missus?" he asked.

"No." Mother moved backward till she was blocking the officer's view.

"Well, then. We'll be off." They went back toward their car. Mother closed the door firmly.

"What were you saying about rituals?" she asked, her voice like steel.

The smell of the policemen lingered in the hallway. Sweat and bay rum.

"Nothing," Doris said. "Nothing at all."

"Well, let's try and get some sleep." Mother stood and grasped the banister with her hand. "Tomorrow will come soon enough."

Doris tossed and turned in the hot bedroom. Where was Douglas right now? she wondered. What was he doing?

Every so often Mother's bedsprings creaked, and

Doris knew neither of them was getting much sleep that night.

Ever since Father had left, life had been different. Douglas had turned troublesome, always fighting. Mother had gotten thinner and smiled less and less. If only, Doris thought, she could find Father and bring him back, life would be like it had been. They wouldn't have to leave their house. Douglas would settle down and go to college. Mother would laugh.

She sat bolt upright in bed.

That was it!

She was going to find her father and bring him back.

Right after she got her brother out of trouble.

Chapter 5

Mother's eyes had dark circles under them the next morning. She splashed cold water on her face at the kitchen sink, turned and pressed her hand into the small of her back. Doris' shirt was already sticking to her back.

"Scorcher," Mother said, standing in the door, looking out over the backyard.

Doris nodded. She drizzled some corn syrup over her oatmeal. "You'll need to find Douglas today," Mother said. "It's Friday, so he'll have to find someplace to stay until tomorrow morning. Do you think he can do that?"

Doris thought of the roadhouses along the river. That was where he must have gone last night after she'd lost sight of him. "I'm sure he can find somewhere."

Mother turned and slumped into a chair at the

table. She sipped listlessly at a cup of coffee. "Too hot for coffee," she said.

"Do you want me to go now?" Doris asked as she put her bowl in the sink.

"Be back before lunch, Doris," Mother said. "We've got to pack up a few things."

Doris backed onto the porch, jumped onto the lawn, crossed to her four-leaf clover patch and fell to her knees. She could use a four-leaf clover today. Shoot! She could use an entire bouquet.

"Doris Stanley, you skedaddle!" Mother hollered from the porch. "Find that brother of yours, like I said."

Doris hustled onto the road. The sun blazed in the sky like a big old ball of fire. Even the birds were staying hidden in the rustling green branches overhead. Doris set off down Lincoln Avenue toward Ford Bathing Beach, thinking she'd maybe take a dip on her way out toward the roadhouses. Johnnie Mullins came striding by, back from the beach.

"Hey, Doris, where are you heading?"

"Find Douglas," Doris muttered. That Johnnie Mullins was just too darn superior, even if he did look like Errol Flynn.

"Where's he at?" Johnnie asked as he pulled his juggling balls out of his pants pocket.

"Dunno," Doris said.

Johnnie started juggling. Doris watched, hypnotized.

"He's hiding down at the river," Johnnie said, keeping his eyes on an imaginary point somewhere above his head. The balls sailed round and round in a steady, hypnotic motion.

"Why're you talking out of the side of your mouth like that?" Doris asked.

"'Cause you never know who might be listening," Johnnie said in a whisper.

Doris glanced around. The street was empty.

"What are you going on about, Johnnie Mullins?"

"Never you mind, Miss Nosy Parker." Johnnie turned and started walking, keeping the balls in the air.

Doris had no choice. She trotted after him. "You know where he is."

"Maybe."

"You better tell me then. My mother wants me to find him."

As they rounded the corner, Doris heard a voice. "Doris!"

She stopped. Johnnie kept juggling.

"Doris, over here!" Doris looked wildly around.

"Pretend you're watching Johnnie juggle."

Doris trained her eyes on Johnnie's hands. "That's right," said the voice. "Now back up. Slowly."

Doris backed slowly toward the bushes. "Okay, you're almost here. Now duck!"

Doris dropped to her knees and gasped as she was pulled under a huge fir tree. Douglas was lying flat on his stomach, pine needles stuck to his hair. His face was grimy and dripping with sweat.

Johnnie Mullins started whistling.

"When Johnnie stops whistling, we know there's trouble," said Douglas.

"What's going on?"

"After I left you last night, I hitched a ride out to the Edgewater Inn. I remember how Father always used to talk about Miss Thomas and what a nice lady she was. I thought she'd let me hang out there for a night. Sure enough, she said it'd be okay, as long as I made myself useful. She put me to work washing dishes. But they raided the place, and I got caught."

"Oh, no!"

"But when they tried to put us in the paddy wagon, someone started shooting." Douglas' face looked a sickly green. "I saw a man get shot, Doris. After that, I ran, and I tell you I've learned something pretty important. I'm never going near this bootlegging business ever again."

Doris shut her eyes and said a word of thanks.

"But now I'm in even bigger trouble than before. Now I'm an escaped fugitive."

"So that's what all this secrecy is about."

Johnnie was whistling "Camp Town Races." *Gonna run all night.*

Douglas scratched his head. "These darn pine needles are killing me."

"They aren't anything compared to what Mother's going to do to you."

Douglas stopped scratching and swiped a hand across his eyes.

For a minute, Doris thought he might be crying. Douglas? Crying? Never.

Gonna run all day.

She patted his arm, and he shrugged her hand off. He blew his nose on the hem of his shirt. Doris glanced away. The musty smell of the dirt rose up her nostrils, choking her. Johnnie continued to whistle.

Bet my money on a bob-tail nag,

"Listen, Douglas. Mother wants you to meet us at the train station on Saturday morning. We're leaving."

Douglas looked at her, his eyes wide. "Leaving?"

"Yeah. Mother's rented the house to Mr. Mullins' brother. We're going to Point Pelee for the entire summer." Now Doris felt like crying.

"You're kidding me!"

"No. She got fired yesterday too."

Douglas smacked his hand against the ground. "Darn this Depression."

Somebody bet on the bay.

The whistling stopped. Doris and Douglas stared at each other.

"Hello, *officer.*" Johnnie's voice was loud and friendly. "Why sure, *officer.* I was just practicing my juggling, that's all."

Doris peeked out from under the branches at two pairs of legs. Johnnie's threadbare trousers moved away. The black-clad legs stood for a long moment. Doris wondered if the legs belonged to one of the policemen who had come to her house last night. At last the black trousers walked off.

"Listen, Doris. Tell Mother I'm all right. I'll sleep out somewhere tonight; maybe I'll hitch a ride out to the country. I'll be at the train station tomorrow morning, like you said."

"At ten o'clock, Mother said."

Doug nodded. "You got anything to eat?"

Doris shook her head. Her own stomach nagged at her. Doug crawled to the edge of the tree. "The coast is clear. I'll see you tomorrow."

Then he was off, the blackened soles of his feet racing across the street and into the grassy field beyond.

Doris rolled out from the branches and sat up.

She brushed herself off and picked the pine needles out of her cotton shirt. Her hands and knees were grimy. Her throat was as dry as the desert. Her empty stomach howled its protest.

But Douglas was safe.

Mother was packing a battered old cardboard suitcase when Doris got home. "Did you find him?"

"Yes."

"Where was he?"

"Hiding under a tree." Doris thought it best to keep the part about the Edgewater Inn, the shooting, the police raid and Douglas' escape from custody for another time.

Mother sank onto the bed. "Thank the Lord."

Doris nodded. She wasn't sure who to thank or what to be thankful for.

That night she lay in her bed for the last time. The moon was too bright for sleep. Doris went to her window and looked out. A movement caught her eye, and she craned her neck. Johnnie Mullins was on his front porch swing. The crickets chirped in time with the slight squeak of the swing as it moved back and forth.

Hold the phone! Johnnie was with a girl. It was that Edith Pitre who lived on Lillian Street. Doris' heart beat a little harder. She craned her neck farther out the window. Is this what Douglas meant by spooning? The low murmur of their voices floated through the summer air.

Doris felt a squishy feeling in the pit of her stomach and a fluttery sensation in the back of her chest. When Johnnie leaned over and kissed Edith, Doris could almost count the hairs on the back of his neck. Doris' tongue tasted salt. And she realized she was crying.

Maybe spending the summer on Point Pelee wasn't going to be so bad after all.

It didn't look like anything about this entire summer was going to be the same, anyway.

Chapter 6

The train pulled into the station, and Doris scanned the platform for a sight of Douglas. The platform was jammed with people, mostly farm workers with wives and children.

"Mr. Mullins has a cousin who is going to pick us up in Leamington," Mother said, as if Doris had asked a question. Her eyes bounced from one group of people to another.

"Don't worry. He'll be here," Doris said, giving Mother's hand a tug.

"I know," Mother said, then with a sudden movement pulled Doris into the shadow of the doorway.

Out of the corner of her eye, Doris saw the flash of a blue uniform. Mother's arm encircled her. "The police," she whispered.

Doris peeked around the corner. It was the two officers who had come to their house!

"What are they doing here?" Mother said. "Surely they have more important criminals than Douglas to catch."

Doris' hand was slippery and hot. She wiped her palms on her knees. The platform was emptying as people piled into the cars. Mother started to pace.

"What will we do if he doesn't make it in time?" Doris asked.

The whistle blasted a warning. The remaining passengers jostled for position.

Mother's pacing became even more frantic. Doris closed her eyes and counted to ten. She thought of the words she'd learned in the last week alone. *Inferno. Ambrosia. Scofflaw.* They didn't help. The pit of her stomach jumped like a butter churn.

"Let's go," Mother said abruptly. She marched forward, pulling Doris by the hand.

"But…"

The police officers appeared beside them.

"Going somewhere?" asked the older man, tipping his hat.

"To visit relatives," Mother replied, pushing Doris ahead of her onto the train. Another passenger held out his hand to help Mother aboard.

"Aaaal aaaaboooooard!" shouted the conductor.

"If we may have a word, ma'am?" said the younger policeman. He didn't tip his hat.

Mother turned and stared the young officer down. "What is it you want?"

"Where is your son, ma'am?"

"I don't know," Mother answered truthfully. "I haven't seen him since Thursday night. All this trouble has been bad for my nerves." She fanned her face with a linen hankie. "And I am taking my daughter to stay with a cousin in Leamington."

The older officer scanned the platform, which was now empty of people.

"All aboard, ma'am," said the conductor.

Mother looked enquiringly at the policemen.

"All right," said the older officer. "But this is serious business. A man was killed on the riverfront two nights ago. Out at the Edgewater. I think your son could be a witness."

Doris closed her eyes. Mother took hold of the conductor's arm for support. The police officers stepped back. "You'd best tell him to turn himself in, ma'am. Some mighty dangerous people are going to be looking for him."

Mother nodded and stepped onto the train. A huge cloud of steam rose from the engine; the train whistle blasted again. The train began its slow chug, chug, chugging motion. Mother sank into a seat as the train rolled out of the station. Doris stared out the window, hoping for a sight of her brother. All that remained were the porters and the two policemen.

"Don't act like you're expecting someone, Doris," Mother said. Her voice trembled.

Doris waved. The older officer lifted his hand. The young officer glared at the disappearing train. Douglas really was a witness to a murder!

"Now what in the world was that all about?" asked a sturdy, smartly dressed woman in the next seat.

"I have no idea," Mother replied sharply. Doris sat down facing her mother and watched Windsor fade from sight. Douglas, where are you? her brain repeated with every turn of the wheels. Doris fidgeted in her seat, wishing she could jump off the train.

"Sit still, Doris," Mother said.

Doris forced herself to sit quietly as the dusty brown city gave way to huge fields of tobacco and tomatoes.

Each time the train stopped, more and more people boarded until it was packed with men in shirtsleeves and women with bundles under their arms and children on their knees. The air filled with many different languages, the smell of onions and sweat. At the first stop outside the city, the train picked up several Negroes. Doris scanned the shacks and gasoline station that made up the whistle-stop.

Mother mopped her face with her handkerchief and opened the top button of her dress. The squat woman next to Mother moved over a seat as another woman asked her to make room.

The train pulled out of the stop, along the grass-grown track.

Then she saw him, a boy, running from behind the gas pumps. A boy running at a gallop, his hair flying back off his face and his feet churning up clouds of dust. A boy running to beat the band.

Doris craned her neck to see. "Mother..." she began. Her heart vaulted to her mouth. The boy stuck out an arm, grabbed hold of the boxcar and hung there, unable to pull himself up. Would he fall beneath the wheels of the train? All at once, arms reached out of the open door and clasped the boy's hand. His feet lifted off the ground, and for one instant he looked like he was flying. More hands reached out to him, taking hold of his shirt, his sleeves, his trousers. Then he disappeared.

Mother was looking out the window, her face stony. Doris chewed her lip and opened her dictionary. She needed a word, any word, but the letters on the page swarmed into a million crawling black insects. Had she just seen what she thought she had? That boy had almost been killed. That boy who looked just like Douglas. Her heart skipped a beat.

The sturdy woman was watching Doris, her eyes small and raisinlike in her doughy face.

Mother sighed and closed her eyes.

Doris smiled at the fat woman, who scowled and turned away. Douglas. He had found them.

Her finger landed on a word. *Optimist.* She continued to read.

One who thinks the best will happen.

If you were a person who believed in signs, thought Doris, this would be a good omen.

"How long will it be until we get to Leamington?" Doris asked.

Mother opened her eyes and mopped her face again. Doris desperately wanted to tell her she'd seen Douglas jump the train, but the squat woman was listening to every word she said.

"A couple of hours."

"Can I go look around?"

Mother nodded and closed her eyes. She looked exhausted. "Don't leave this car, though."

Doris stood. She might jump out of her skin if she had to sit still for two whole hours. She patted Mother's knee as she went by. "Be an optimist," she said in a low voice.

Mother opened her eyes again. Doris winked.

The other woman raised her eyebrows.

Doris patrolled the car. One of the passengers

had a ukulele and was playing a tune Doris recognized about a big rock candy mountain.

The soft voice and plunking of the ukulele strings caused a few of the other passengers to join in the song. Doris sat on the arm of one of the seats and listened.

Eventually, the train slowed down. The fields gave way to streets and rows of wooden houses.

"Leamington!" shouted the conductor, and the passengers gathered their belongings. Mother rose and picked up the cardboard suitcase.

Doris peered out the window, looking for Douglas.

"What are you looking for?" Mother asked, following the line of Doris' vision.

"Nothing," Doris answered when the squat lady pushed up behind them. The crowd jostled and pushed its way off the train, to the end of the platform, and dispersed in many directions.

A tall man with sandy hair, wearing coveralls, approached Mother.

"Mrs. Stanley?" he asked. He held his sweat-stained hat in two hands in front of him.

Mother nodded. "Are you Giles Mullins?"

"That I am. Ronald asked me to drive you to the Point." He nodded and nodded and nodded. His head bobbed up and down like a baby's with no neck muscles.

"Mother," Doris said in a low voice.

"Not now, Doris," Mother said, handing her suitcase to Mr. Mullins' cousin.

"But it's important."

Mother turned. "What is it?"

"I think I saw Douglas jump the train," Doris whispered. "But I didn't see him get off."

Mr. Mullins had ears like a dog, Doris figured, because he chimed right in.

"Them tramps don't ride the train into the station, little girl. No sir. They jump off when the train slows down. No sense in getting caught." He nodded at the constable standing by the baggage pickup.

"How do you know it was him?" Mother asked, her voice wobbly.

"Saw his face, clear as day."

"Why didn't you say something before?"

"That lady."

Mother swallowed hard. She turned to Mr. Mullins. "It's my son. He was supposed to meet us at the train station, but we had to leave without him."

Mr. Mullins slapped his hat back on his head. "My cousin mentioned something about this son of yours," he drawled. "I think I know where we can find him."

He led them to his beat-up old pickup truck and put their suitcase in the back. Mother sat up front and Doris sat on the suitcase to keep it from bumping out of the open back. Dirt flew everywhere, clogging her hair, her nose and her eyes. They drove past the Heinz factory, into which flowed an endless chain of buckets overflowing with tomatoes. A vinegary smell pierced the dusty air, sharp, astringent.

"That's where they make ketchup," Doris heard Mr. Mullins shouting at Mother.

After a drive of fifteen minutes, during which Doris almost pitched out the back of the truck five times, they turned off onto another dirt road that led to the lake. After another minute or two, they rattled to a stop, and Mr. Mullins jumped down from the driver's seat.

"You ladies wait here," he said as he strode off in the direction of campfire smoke.

Mother peered anxiously after him, and Doris jumped down and trotted down the trail.

"Doris!" Mother called.

"Be right back," Doris shouted over her shoulder. She wasn't going to wait around to see what was going to happen next, no sir!

The campfire smoke was rising from behind a stand of tall pine trees. The pungent smell of pine needles reminded Doris of finding Douglas under the tree. Her heart hammered against her ribs as she caught up with Mr. Mullins.

He smiled at her. "Maybe it's just as well you came along," he said. "Point him out to me if you see him."

They rounded the stand of trees, and Doris' jaw hung open in amazement. An entire town was set up around a group of tents and smoldering fires. Black iron cooking pots hung from sticks over the fires, and barefoot children scampered through the dirt chasing an old barrel wheel.

"See him anywhere?" asked Mr. Mullins.

Doris scanned the faces. They looked back at her, thin cheeked and hollow eyed. She stepped slightly behind Mr. Mullins. He put his hand on her shoulder.

"You want to wait back at the truck?" he asked.

Some of the smaller children had come boldly forward, staring at the strangers.

"Any new arrivals?" Mr. Mullins asked the oldest child, a boy around seven.

A tall, scrawny man detached himself from the crowd at the campfire and joined the children. Mr. Mullins and he walked off to one side and talked in low voices.

"What's that?" a ragged girl of around four asked Doris. She pointed at the book in Doris' hand.

Doris looked down in surprise. In her haste, she'd forgotten to leave her dictionary in the truck.

"A book that tells you the meaning of words," she said.

The girl's eyes flickered upward to Doris' ponytail. "You got ribbons," she said in a reverential tone.

Doris pulled the bow out of her hair. She hated ribbons; Mother had made her wear her best clothes on the train. She held the bit of silk out to the little girl, whose eyes went round as flapjacks.

"Here," Doris said. "Want this?"

The child nodded. The other children pressed closer, angling for a look at this bearer of gifts.

"Let me tie up your hair," Doris said, grasping the child's bony shoulders and turning her around. Doris scooped up a handful of the lank hair and fashioned a bow from the satin ribbon. "There," she said. "You look beautiful."

The child fingered the ribbon, rubbing the satiny end against her cheek. Her dull eyes shone.

"What's your name?" Doris asked.

"Her name's Annie," said a stooped woman as she grasped the child's arm and pulled her away. She coughed, spat into a filthy handkerchief and looked at Doris through narrowed eyes.

Mr. Mullins and the man walked past. Doris started after them, but a small hand slipped into hers, holding her back. She stopped. The ragged child smiled a close-lipped smile.

"Come with me," she said.

Doris looked at Mr. Mullins' retreating back. She pulled at her hand, but the child wouldn't let go. Mr. Mullins and the man had turned a corner, the dust they had kicked into the air the only sign they had passed that way. The child tugged again, more insistently this time.

"He wants to see you."

Doris looked over the child's head. The old woman moved forward again and gestured for Doris to do as the child said.

"Who?" asked Doris.

The woman jerked her chin at a dirty tent. Doris followed the child to its flapping door. The smell of dirt, grease and wood smoke was overwhelming. She looked back over her shoulder for some sight of Mr. Mullins, but he was long gone. The child fingered her ribbon and ducked through the tent door. With one final look at the trees where she had last seen Mr. Mullins, Doris took a deep breath and followed.

"Douglas!"

Her brother was lying on the ground, his foot propped on a stack of threadbare blankets.

"I heard voices. Who's that with you?" he asked in a hoarse voice.

"Mr. Mullins' cousin. What happened?"

"Sprained my ankle jumping off that darned train. You sure he's not the police or something?"

"Sure, I'm sure. He met us at the train, just like Mr. Mullins said he would. Seems real nice to me."

Douglas licked his dry lips and winced. Doris could see where his ankle was swollen to twice the size of his other one.

"You okay, Douglas?" Doris asked as she knelt at his side. "You don't look too good."

"I'll be all right. Where's Mother?"

"Waiting in Mr. Mullins' truck. How'd you get here?"

"Jumped the train just outside town. Fred brought me here."

"You mean the man talking to Mr. Mullins?" Doris asked.

Douglas nodded. The voices of the two men came closer. "They're coming!" Douglas whispered.

"It's all right, I tell you," Doris whispered back.

Mr. Mullins and Fred knelt down at the entrance to the tent. "So, you're young Douglas," said Mr. Mullins, holding out his hand.

"Yessir," Doug said. He reached up and shook Mr. Mullins' hand.

"Well, you had your ma good and worried. I think you'd best come along with us. Can you walk?"

"Not too well."

"Here." He turned his handshake into a yank and pulled Douglas to his feet. "Doris, how about you get under his other arm and help hold him up."

With Douglas leaning on them, they made their way up the bumpy trail. The little girl ran along beside them, her hair bouncing on her back. The ribbon already looked soiled.

The child stopped at the end of the path, stuck her grubby fingers into her mouth and waved. Doris waved back. The child watched until they rounded the bend.

Mother jumped down from the truck the moment she saw them.

"Lord, Douglas," she gathered him into a giant hug. "It's been days since I've seen you."

Doris could have sworn she saw a tear glisten on Doug's cheek.

"We'd best get moving," Mr. Mullins said, climbing up behind the wheel. "Doesn't pay to stick around anywhere too long. Something could be gaining on you."

Douglas stretched out in the back of the truck along with Doris. He closed his eyes and winced each time the truck bounced over a bump in the rutted road. His face was thinner, and dirt was caked into the squint lines around his eyes.

"Boy, I'm tired, Doris," he said through clenched

teeth. There was some dried spittle in the corner of his mouth. "It sure is a mess, isn't it?"

"What do you mean?" Doris asked.

"Father's being gone and all," Douglas said. "Life sure isn't the same as it used to be."

"You know, Douglas," Doris said, "I was reading somewhere..."

"You're always reading," Douglas interrupted, opening his eyes and staring at the sky. "What good's reading when we got to eat?"

"Reading teaches you new ways of thinking about things, Doug," said Doris.

"Can't eat books," he said with finality.

"Like I was saying," Doris continued, "I was reading somewhere, 'Give a man a fish, he's got fish for a day. Teach a man to fish, he's got fish for life.'"

Doug stared at her hard. "Sometimes you're downright scary, you know that?"

The truck turned down a long driveway. Mr. Mullins shouted over his shoulder. "We're just stopping at the house to pick up a tent. My cousin asked me to lend you a few camping things."

Mother fanned herself with her hat. Insects buzzed in the bushes. Hollyhocks drooped in the sun. "Go help Mr. Mullins, Doris," she said.

Doris trotted down the dirt drive toward the barn. "Got this stuff for my son when he was ten,"

Mr. Mullins said. "Lost him in the Great War." He swiped his brow with the back of his hand.

Doris sneezed in all the dust.

They loaded the tent, some sleeping bags and a few dishes into the back of the truck beside Douglas. At the sight of all the camping gear, he perked up.

By the time they reached the Point, it was after three o'clock. Doris' stomach grumbled angrily as they unloaded the truck in a wooded spot away from the official campsites.

"How come we have to pitch camp way back here?" she asked Mr. Mullins.

"Best to stay away from the authorities just now," he said. Mother's mouth was set in a hard line.

Douglas looked around him with interest. "I bet I can catch a rabbit for dinner," he said.

When the tent was set up and the sleeping bags put inside, Mr. Mullins pulled a picnic basket of groceries from behind his seat.

"Here's a few things to get you folks started," he said, handing the basket to Mother. "You can leave off trapping rabbits for today, anyway."

Doris' mouth watered at the sight of jars of preserved peaches, pickles and a smoked ham. She hadn't seen so much good food in months.

Mr. Mullins tipped his hat to Mother.

"I don't know how to thank you for your help," she said.

He held up his hand. His head bobbed on his long neck. He smiled a shy smile that was gone practically before it arrived. "No need, ma'am. Glad to help. Times like these, we all got to stick together." He turned to Doris and squatted down. "You've been a big help, little lady. You keep an eye on that brother of yours."

Douglas glared at them from where he was trying to start a fire.

"Yessir," Doris said.

Mother walked Mr. Mullins to the truck. Doris heard him say, "I'll check back in a week or so. See if you need anything."

Mother waved until the truck was out of sight. Then she came back to the campfire.

"Why are you flushed, Mother?" asked Doris.

Mother put her hand against her cheek and spoke sternly. "Hush, now, Doris."

Doris looked carefully. No doubt about it. Mother's face was flaming red! Douglas seemed to have recovered some energy. He hobbled around, picking up kindling wood, hauling out an old black cast-iron frying pan, slicing off hunks of smoked ham and setting them in the pan over a ring of stones. Mother pulled out some tin dishes and a coffeepot, and Doris' mouth watered like Niagara Falls.

"Look!" Mother said. "He's put in some real coffee and sugar!"

It felt like Christmas morning. Never had Doris been so hungry. Never had food tasted so good. Doug was safe. They were together.

Except for Father.

Doris swallowed a lump in her throat.

Why was it that she could never get all the pieces to fit like they were supposed to? Why couldn't she just fix things once and for all?

Chapter 7

The sound of birds woke Doris when the sun was still low in the sky. She scratched at her arm and noticed over a dozen mosquito bites. Beside her, Mother stirred restlessly in her sleep.

It was damp and musty smelling in the tent, and Doris had a stiff neck. She looked around sleepily.

Douglas wasn't in his sleeping bag!

She sat up, wide-awake. Her heart pounded, keeping time with the hammering of a woodpecker in a tree beside their campsite. She crawled to the tent door, just in time to see Douglas limping down the path with a giant perch on the end of his fishing line.

"Look what I caught for breakfast," he said, his eyes shining.

Doris expelled her breath. Maybe camping would be good for Douglas. Keep him away from rum-running.

The smell of fish frying brought Mother out of the tent. "Lord, did you hear those birds?" She walked over to the fire and warmed her hands. She pushed a few stray wisps of hair into her bun.

"I found a great swimming spot," Douglas said as he flipped the fish. Its skin was golden brown. He threw a few chopped-up potatoes into the pan. "And there's an apple orchard nearby. We can go look after breakfast."

Doris wondered how long it would take for the hole in her stomach to fill up. Maybe after a whole summer on the Point, where they could eat fish and apples to their heart's content, she wouldn't feel hungry anymore. She glanced at Mother.

"That's a good idea, Douglas. Mr. Mullins put some sugar and lard in that basket. I could make a Brown Betty."

Maybe Point Pelee was actually heaven, Doris thought.

Douglas had fashioned himself a crutch out of a piece of wood. "Here, Pipsqueak," he said, handing Doris the frying pan. "Make yourself useful."

No doubt about it. He was acting just like his old self.

Doris and Douglas hauled the frying pan and dishes through the trees to the water's edge. Lake Erie stretched out as far as the eye could see.

"It's as big as an ocean, Doug," said Doris, shielding her eyes from the sun, now high in the eastern sky.

Giant birds floated on the air currents above them.

"Turkey vultures," Doug said, nodding upward. "Great soaring birds."

The air thrummed with noise: birds singing, frogs croaking, insects humming. Behind Doris, the branches crashed.

"Run!" yelled a boy as he burst out of the bushes and raced along the beach, followed by a woman.

"The park ranger," she shouted as she ran by. "Hide!"

Douglas hobbled to the thickest part of the bushes. "Bring the dishes," he hissed as he motioned for Doris to hurry. She grabbed the sandy pan and jumped into the thicket.

"Don't you think that boy looked familiar?" she said, looking at Douglas.

"Shhhh!" he answered, pointing through the branches and leaves.

Doris held her breath. A tall man came striding down the path, stopped at the sand, then continued down the beach the way the woman and boy had gone.

“We’d better tell Mother,” Douglas said, standing.

Were people ever going to stop chasing them?

Mother’s face hardened when Douglas told her about the ranger. “Just keep out of his way,” she said as she draped the sleeping bags over a nearby rock to air. “We’ve got no choice but to stay here for the summer. It’s up to the two of you to make sure there’s no trouble.” She looked directly at Douglas.

“Yes, ma’am,” Douglas said, his face flushing bright red.

“Want to show me the swimming spot?” Doris asked, putting her hand on Douglas’ shoulder.

He struggled to his feet and nodded.

The beach was filling up with people. Children chased a ball along the waves. Mothers watched from blankets, waving at the little ones if they got too close to the water.

Doris shivered as the cold water lapped at her ankles. Douglas plunged through the waves, hopping on his good foot.

“Watch for the undertow!” yelled the boy they’d seen running up the beach.

Douglas waved back. He had turned on his back and was floating.

“Is that you, Pete Long?” Doris asked.

"Doris Stanley," he said. "What in blazes are you doing here?"

"Camping," Doris mumbled. Pete was younger than she was. He lived two blocks over in a house full of older brothers. Ruffians, the lady next door called them.

"Me too," Pete said. "My mother sent me away this summer so she wouldn't have to feed me. I was too young to work, so I had to go stay with my aunt. Only problem is, she lost her job so now we're camping because we didn't have anywhere else to go." He pointed at Doug with a stubby finger. "Better tell him to watch out for the undertow."

"What undertow?"

"Terrible undertow," Pete said. "Boy drowned off the end of the point, just last week."

"Douglas!" Doris yelled. Again, he waved.

"Where're you camped?" asked Pete, sitting down and scooping the sand into piles over his bare feet.

"Out back of the orchard," Doris said.

"We're near there," Pete chattered. "We're squatting, just like you."

"How do you know we're squatting?" Doris said, dropping her gaze to where Pete sat. He was now up to his neck in sand.

"Saw you come in last night. Besides, no one camps that far back unless they're squatting. The regular campsites are way over there." He pointed toward the main road.

"So?" Doris asked.

"So you got to stay out of sight of that ranger. Most of them don't care too much. But that one! Boy, oh boy! He'd as soon turn you in as look at you." Pete closed his eyes and sighed. "Sun sure feels good."

"How old are you?" Doris asked.

"Eight. You?"

"Ten. Don't you mind running away from the ranger?"

"It's all in the way you look at it," Pete said, squinting up at her through the sun. "Some folks might be shamed of it. Me, I see it as an adventure."

Douglas hopped out of the water and flopped down beside them. Pete sat up, showering sand all over Douglas' wet skin. He looked like he'd been dipped in sugar.

"Thanks for the warning earlier," Douglas said. "You live in Windsor, don't you?"

"Yep," Pete said.

"Doris thought she saw you someplace."

"Sure," said Pete. "Say, have you ever been to a palmist?"

"What's that?" Doris asked.

"Someone who tells the future," said Pete. "There's

a lady living in a tent over by the cannery. Her sister is a palmist over in Put-in-Bay."

Douglas nodded like he understood everything Pete was saying.

"Put-in-Bay?" Doris repeated.

"That's an island on the other side of the lake." Pete lowered his voice and looked around. "I stowed away on the steamer last week and got all the way to the United States."

"Really?" Doris asked, glancing at Douglas. That Pete could sure spin a tall tale. Doris didn't like the way Douglas' eyes were riveted on Pete's face.

Pete squinted into the sun and said, "Say, you know something?"

Douglas shook his head. He was watching a boy casting a fishing line from the shore.

"I saw a man over in Put-in-Bay, looked a lot like your pa."

"What?" Doris stared into Pete's eyes. Was he telling the truth?

"How would you know what our father looked like?" asked Douglas.

"My pa used to work with him when they were building some gardens in Jackson Park in Windsor. I skipped school and tagged along a few times. My pa never cared much for schooling. But your pa always gave me a talking to. Told me I ought to take my education seriously."

"Let's go, Douglas," Doris said. She didn't like the look on Douglas' face. "Mother will be wondering where we are." She tugged on her brother's arm. Douglas shook her off.

"That sounds like something Father would say, all right. Doesn't it, Doris?" Doug turned to her, his face hopeful.

"You children can be anything you want with a good education. You've got opportunities that I never had. Don't throw them away." Father was sitting at the old well-scrubbed kitchen table. He was adding figures on a long scrap of paper. It was the beginning of the hard times, and he was entering a contest that had a prize of a thousand dollars. Father was as smart as they come, but he never had much luck in life. The contest turned out to be a scam, and it took his last dollar to enter. It hadn't been long after that that she'd gotten up one morning and found Father gone and Mother crying.

Doris shook the memory away. "I don't know, Douglas. What would he be doing over there? Why wouldn't he come home?"

Doug stood up. His shadow fell across her face. "Doris Stanley, you're always pooh-poohing everything. You're just a stupid scaredy-cat. You won't ever admit when something's possible!" Doug pitched a stone into the water.

"Well, answer me, then!" Doris yelled. She started to shake. "If he's so close by, why wouldn't he just come home?"

"I don't know!" Douglas stalked to the tree line. "But maybe I'm going to find out." He disappeared down the trail.

Pete stood up awkwardly. "Well, I guess I shouldn't have said anything."

"Hold on, Pete." Doris stood to face him. "Where exactly did you see this man?"

"He was working one of the entertainment booths they have over there. Sitting behind the rifle range."

"Pete!" yelled a woman standing at the tree line. "Come pick berries."

"Well, I'd better get," said Pete, shaking himself like a wet dog, spraying sand in all directions.

Pete brushed the last bit of sand off his arm and mock-saluted. "See you around," he called back as he disappeared into the trees.

Douglas was sitting on a fallen log halfway down the trail, whittling in silence.

Doris sat down beside him, wishing she knew what to say.

For a long time Douglas ignored her. Then he said, "Do you believe people can really tell the future?" His voice was steady, not strained and high pitched like when he'd shouted at her down by the beach.

"Don't see how they can," Doris answered. "Don't see how it's possible."

"Still. Wouldn't you like to know what's going to happen to us?"

"Douglas!" Doris stood up. The sounds of the forest stopped. The sun beat down on them through the dappled leaves.

Douglas didn't look up. He picked some berries from a wild mulberry bush. Popped one in his mouth.

Doris wanted to scream, but she held her tongue. Douglas popped another berry in his mouth.

"If you try anything funny, Mother will die!"

"Don't be silly. I'm not going to do anything."

He stuck out his tongue, which was as purple as ink.

Mother called from the clearing. "Just in time for lunch."

Doris caught the smell of apples and cinnamon. Mother must have made a Brown Betty, just like she'd said.

"After lunch we can come back here and pick the rest of these mulberries," said Douglas.

Doris' hands unclenched. He was telling the truth. He wasn't going to do anything foolish.

So why didn't she feel better?

Chapter 8

A light rain pattered on the canvas tent, and outside the morning sun was shrouded in haze. Douglas' sleeping bag was empty, but Doris had gotten used to that in the three weeks they'd been there. As soon as his ankle had healed, he began a routine of fishing every morning, leaving long before she or Mother opened their eyes.

Doris liked the sound of the rain and the soft whoosh of Mother's regular breathing. Doris patted her stomach and smiled in the dull early morning light. She sure did like having enough to eat! She stretched her hands way over her head. What might Douglas bring home this morning?

Her fingers brushed her dictionary and she rolled over onto her stomach and pulled the book closer. She closed her eyes, flipped open the cover and stabbed a finger onto the page. She opened her eyes and looked. There it was! Her word for the day.

Cozen.

Now that's a mighty fine word, Doris thought. She checked the pronunciation guide. Sounds like "cousin." *To deceive by petty trick or fraud.* Yessir, Doris thought. That's a mighty fine word indeed.

She lay there savoring the word, rolling it around in her mouth, letting it trickle over her tongue like maple walnut ice cream. The rain stopped.

The sound of whistling tickled her eardrum. Douglas was on his way back. Mother rolled over in her sleeping bag and opened her eyes. Doris and Mother smiled at each other. Birds chattered in the warmth of the morning as the sun broke through the clouds.

"Come on, you sleepyheads!" called Douglas from outside the tent. "Got a couple of nice pickerel this morning." Soon Doris' taste buds were jumping at the smell of coffee and frying fish.

The clearing came to life. Beautiful orange-and-black butterflies dipped through the air like miniature marionettes. Squirrels chattered in the branches. Ill-tempered blue jays scolded as they chased each other through the trees.

"Was talking to a fellow down at the beach this morning," Doug said through a mouthful of food.

Doris glanced at Mother. She didn't even tell Douglas to chew with his mouth shut. Doris frowned.

"He said those butterflies go all the way to Mexico during the winter. Imagine that! Looks like a stiff wind would blow them to Mars."

Doris studied her mother as Douglas wiped his mouth on the back of his sleeve. No reaction! Doris took another bite of fish and turned her attention back to her brother.

"He said something else mighty interesting."

Doris leaned forward, grabbed the last bit of fried bread and shoved it in her mouth. Mother didn't scold her. Doris chewed slowly, enjoying the pilfered food less than she had expected to.

"Yes sir," Douglas continued. "Man said that coming across Lake Superior, those butterflies suddenly make a strange turn. No one can figure out why they would zigzag that way, because it adds all kinds of extra miles to their journey."

"So why do they do it?" Doris asked, turning her eyes away from Mother.

"No one knows for sure," Doug said, brushing crumbs from his lap. "But there's one theory."

"What's that?"

"Well, some people think those old butterflies are remembering a glacier that used to be in the very spot where they make their strange turn. They think that the memory of that iceberg is in the brain of every butterfly that's ever going to fly across that lake. That they are born knowing that glacier used to be there."

"Don't believe it," said Doris.

"Well, Doris," Douglas said, "there are lots of things people can't explain. Doesn't mean they aren't real."

"Like palmists?" Doris said, putting her plate down and not even caring that there was still a piece of fish to eat.

"Maybe," Doug said.

Doris glanced at Mother. Surely she was going to say something!

Mother's eyes focused on them. She seemed to have dragged herself back from a long way away. "Goodness," she said, glancing at the sky. "Sun's climbing. I've got to get dressed."

"Something wrong, Mother?" Doris asked.

"Mr. Mullins is coming to get me this morning. I have an important matter to attend to in Leamington. He telephoned the store last night and left a message with Ida saying that he'd be here at nine this morning." She stood and put a pan of water on the fire to heat. "First, I have to give myself a wash. Mercy!" She scooped her hair up off her neck and ran a washcloth all around her face and chin. "I haven't had a good wash in weeks!"

Doris had so many questions that she didn't know where to start. She turned around in time to see Douglas watching her, his face stony.

Mother disappeared into the tent. Her voice was muffled as she changed her clothes. "You two are going to have to stay here alone today." Her voice changed. "Promise me you won't get into any trouble."

"Why didn't you tell us about this yesterday?" Doris asked.

"Because Ida didn't come by until last night after you were asleep," said Mother.

"What kind of important matter?" Doris persisted.

"We'll discuss it when I get back."

Douglas threw a stick at a tree. It thumped off the trunk and ricocheted back at him, narrowly missing his head.

Doris' head spun from her mother's voice inside the tent to where her brother stood, staring at the path toward the water. She started to hiccup.

"What are you planning?" Doris hiccuped at her brother.

"Quiet down, Pipsqueak."

Mother emerged from the tent wearing her church clothes. Her hair was tied up neatly, the way she wore it for special occasions. Douglas smothered the fire with sand. Doris wished she knew what to do next.

A sputtering car engine sent the squirrels flying like trapeze artists through the overhead branches. Mr. Mullins' truck appeared around the bend. Mother gathered her things together and started down the path to meet him.

Doris ran after her. "When are you coming back?" she asked.

Mother turned around and put her hand on Doris' shoulder. "Sometime tonight. You watch out for your brother."

Doris shook her head. Something was terribly wrong! Mother couldn't just leave without telling them why. The hiccups came faster. "Why are you going?"

Mother's face was serious, her eyes gray and deep. "Your grandfather," Mother said, "my father, in Alberta..." She hesitated, as if trying to decide whether or not to go on.

"The one you never talk to?" Doris asked. She remembered her parents quarreling late one Christmas Eve. Her father had shouted that he wasn't taking anything from the Dillon family. Not now. Not ever. Mother had cried until Father's voice had softened. Doris had never met her grandparents.

Mother nodded. She patted Doris' back. The hiccups were coming faster and faster, threatening to knock her off her feet.

Mother took a deep breath and continued, "I wrote to ask if we could go there and live. Don't look like that, Doris," she said. "In times like these, we do what we have to do."

Doris was hiccuping so hard that she couldn't speak. When had Mother cooked this up?

Mother gave her a quick hug and smoothed her hair one more time. "He's arrived in Leamington," she said. "And I have to go talk to him."

Doris gasped, shocking the hiccups right out of her system. Grandfather was in Leamington?

"What about Father?" Doris stammered.

Mother's hands shook as she clutched her pocketbook. "I don't know where he is, Doris. We can't manage to stay together as a family unless we do this." She raised her chin. "I expect you and Douglas to understand." Doris' knees crumpled under her the way a log turned to ash in the campfire. She collapsed in the dirt. Mother's shoulders looked as stiff as tent poles as she walked toward Mr. Mullins' truck. Douglas sat down beside Doris.

"I heard what Mother told you."

Doris sat, too stunned to speak.

"I'm not standing for it," Douglas said. "I'm not moving to Alberta."

"What choice do you have?"

"I've got plenty of choices. In fact," Douglas said, standing and briskly brushing his hands on his pants, "I'm making one of those choices right now."

Doris didn't like the sound of that. She struggled to her feet and stared her brother in the eye. "Just what's that supposed to mean?"

"It means I'm going to Put-in-Bay to see if Pete really saw Father."

Doris' heart started doing double Dutch inside her chest. "How're you going to get there?"

"There's a boat that leaves Pelee Island after lunch."

"How do you expect to get to Pelee Island?"

"On Mr. LaPierre's fishing boat."

"He'll let you go?"

"I'll stow away."

"Doug! That sounds dangerous."

"Sounds like you should mind your own business," Douglas snapped as he put a few apples in his pocket. "Gotta go."

He didn't look back as he ran down the path toward the wharf.

If he didn't make her so mad, Doris figured, she'd cry. As it was, she was so riled up she could spit fire.

Fuming, she crawled into the tent and pulled on an old pair of pants and a fishing hat.

Now she'd have to go too, just to make sure he stayed out of trouble. Whether he wanted her to or not.

Chapter 9

Only one fishing boat was still at the dock. All the others had left for the open water at daybreak. Doris crouched behind a bush and watched her brother. Douglas made a big show of fishing off the dock. As soon as Mr. LaPierre went ashore to speak to some men, he slipped into the hold. Doris jumped out from her hiding place and ran onto the dock. Without a backward glance she jumped onto the deck of the boat. She crouched down against the fishy-smelling boards and held her breath. No one yelled, "What the heck do you think you're doing?" so she gulped some air into her screaming lungs, then crawled to the steps and down into the hold.

The look on Douglas' face was worth the price of admission! He gawped and stared and started to yammer.

The sound of creaking boards cut him short. Footsteps pounded across the deck overhead. The boat's engine sputtered to life, and the rocking motion of the waves made Doris' stomach heave. "You're looking a little green around the gills," Douglas said. "Don't you dare upchuck on me."

Doris ran a hand over her clammy forehead. Maybe this wasn't such a good idea after all! Douglas pulled her back behind a pile of crates.

"If they discover us, they'll probably throw us in jail," he warned.

The boat flipped and flopped over the waves like a fish on the line. Breakfast rose in Doris' throat, but she choked it back down. Douglas watched her with disgust.

"Girls!" he muttered. "What'd you have to meddle for? Now you're probably going to get us both caught."

Doris couldn't answer. She was too busy keep-ing her fried fish and bread in her stomach. She drew her legs up to her chest and rested her forehead on her knees.

A waterfall of fish tumbled down a chute along with the rich smell of dirt and the lake. The boat rocked and Douglas pulled Doris closer. A man's feet appeared on the steps and, one after the other, two men thundered down the steps. They began flipping and sorting fish according to their size and packing them in crates of ice.

"Is Thompson meeting us at the island?" grunted one of the men as he heaved a large fish onto a pile. His cloth cap covered one eye and he had a weathered face.

"Said he would," answered LaPierre.

"Think we got enough to make it look like a fishing trip?"

"Yeah, we got enough."

The men went back upstairs. Doug was white as a ghost.

"What's the matter?" Doris whispered.

"I thought it was funny, them leaving so long after the other fishermen," he said.

"What do you mean?"

Doug pried one of the crates open. "It's liquor." He sank onto his knees. "They're bootleggers!"

Doris blinked. Bootleggers?

"They'll kill us if they find us here," Doug said. "I saw what these guys do when I was in Windsor."

"You really see them shoot someone, Douglas?"

Douglas' face turned hard. "Shot each other like they were nothing more than skunks, Doris," he said. "We gotta get out of here!"

Doris peeked out the porthole. "How? We're miles from land."

"We're going to have to swim in."

"We can't swim that far!"

"We're going to have to jump ship as soon's we get a chance." Douglas peered out the window. "Hush!" he said suddenly, his head cocked to one side as he listened to the movements on the deck overhead.

The rocking of the boat lessened and Doris' stomach stopped complaining. They had chugged into a shady cove.

"As soon as we're two hundred feet from shore, we're getting out of here," Douglas said. "Can you do it?"

Doris closed her eyes and tried not to think of Billy McKenzie when his mother fished him out of the Detroit River.

The boat rocked to a stop.

"Why are they stopping?" Doris whispered.

"They're probably waiting for a signal of some kind," Doug replied.

Doug crept to the stairs. "What are you doing?" Doris said.

"Come on!" Douglas beckoned her forward. "We've got to go now!"

Doris scrambled to the steps and followed her brother's heels as they disappeared above deck. He crouched at the top until she got to the top step. "Jump!" he said.

Doris didn't stop to think. She swung one leg over the railing, then the other, then jumped. She felt Douglas land beside her. The cold water iced her toes and shocked the last of the seasickness right out of her. The two of them clung to the side of the boat.

"Do you think they heard us?" Doris asked.

"Doesn't look like it," Douglas said. A cautious smile crept over his face. "Follow me."

Without a sound he pushed off from the boat. Doris swam in his wake. Once in a while she glanced back over her shoulder to see if the men had noticed anything. All she could hear was the sound of laughter and the occasional beer bottle as it hit the water.

"Looks like they're planning to tie one on," Doug said as he and Doris staggered out of the water. "Lucky for us." They made their way quickly up a small hill to the nearest bushes. "We've got to stay out of sight until they leave," Douglas said.

Once they were well hidden, Doris asked, "How are we going to get to Put-in-Bay?"

"Pete told me that a ferry leaves from the other side of the island in about an hour. They'll be gone by then."

"How do you know?"

"Bootleggers never hang around too long. They don't want to get caught."

A light flashed from a cove down the shore.

"There!" Doug said. "See that?" The light flashed again. Three long, three short, three long. "That's a signal."

A boat pushed off from the shore. The cases that Doris and Douglas had hidden behind were transferred to the smaller boat. It sped off across the water, heading for the American side.

"See that boat?" Douglas said, pointing after it. "It belongs to Gordon Thompson, the slickest bootlegger this side of the lake."

"How do you know?" asked Doris again.

"Never you mind, Pipsqueak. I just do."

The sun was almost directly overhead. Old LaPierre was dozing in the sun, his cloth cap pulled down over his eyes.

"Doesn't look like they plan to leave any time soon," Doris said.

"Come on," Douglas grunted. "Don't think they're in any condition to notice us anyhow."

A Coast Guard boat appeared suddenly on the horizon. The bootleggers sprang into action, but they were too late. The Coast Guard pulled up and men with guns boarded the fishing boat.

"What's going on?" Doris whispered.

"Looks like the Coast Guard is searching the boat. Let's get out of here!" Douglas tugged at her arm.

"Where are we going?" Doris asked.

"To the steamer," Doug said. Flies buzzed around them as they crossed the dusty pathways to the ferry dock. Doris' clothes were wet from the swim and chafed against her thighs. She wished she'd just stayed home. But someone had to look out for Douglas. She stared at his back. It seemed to be getting harder and harder to stick to her promise. They made their way along dusty trails past fields of tobacco.

"Pete said the steamer leaves from the west dock. We just need to follow the shoreline as best we can. Island's small," Douglas said reassuringly. "It's probably only half a mile to the dock."

"How are we going to get on the steamer without anyone knowing?" Doris said as she panted after her brother. Sweat dripped off her chin.

"Pete told me what to do," Douglas said.

The dock was busy. Many people were waiting for the steamer. Two men were standing to one side, talking. "This place has no funs," said one, wiping his brow.

The other looked longingly at the people boarding the steamer. "No. No funs at all."

Douglas motioned for Doris to follow. "Those men work at the quarry," he said. "Italians."

At the end of the quay, Douglas stopped. "You two kids!" yelled a large man. "Get out of there!"

Doug waved and made as if to go back the way he had come. The man swung his attention to two ladies who were about to board the steamer. Doug stopped and edged backward toward the deck. He picked up a piece of luggage and marched on board. Doris did the same. A porter just inside the door motioned them toward the baggage hold. Doug dragged Doris into a storage room. It was so hot Doris could barely breathe.

Eventually the steamer pushed away from the quay.

"How long will it take?" Doris asked. She fanned herself with her cap.

"Pete said it only takes an hour."

Through a tiny peephole in the wall, Doris could see well-dressed people sitting in white wicker chairs in the stern. Darkness had begun to creep in over the lake, bringing with it cooler air. The steamer slowed its pace and drifted in to the pier, stopping with a soft bump.

"We've got to run for it," Douglas said. Doris stood. Her legs wobbled under her. "Feet, don't fail me now," Douglas said, grinning at her. They tiptoed out of the storage room and onto the deck. "Pete said to mingle with the crowd until you hit the gangplank, then skedaddle." They followed the women, attaching themselves to their skirt tails. A deckhand was nodding goodbye. He looked hard at Doris and Douglas and started forward.

Douglas shot out of the crowd like an arrow. Doris' legs seethed with sudden energy. They zigzagged through the departing passengers, darting around deckhands who pushed wheelbarrows and hauled luggage.

"Stop!" yelled the deckhand. The boards vibrated underfoot as he pounded after them.

"Faster!" Doug shouted over his shoulder as he picked up speed. Doris was drawn along in his wake. People stepped aside to let them pass. They ran down the pier, under a string of colored lights that blinked a cheery welcome and into the darkness. Douglas ran with the instincts of a homing pigeon, with Doris flying along behind. They left the harbor lights and ran past a row of stalls. Doug ducked behind the test-your-strength booth and caught his breath.

"We're here, Doris!" He smiled and smacked his knee. "I can't believe we made it!"

"Neither can I," Doris said. She was cramped, hot and thirsty. "Don't know why you're in such a good mood. I don't see anyone who looks like Father."

"Give it time, Pipsqueak. We just got here." Doug looked around, his eyes glittering at all the lights and activity.

The sound of music wafted in on the breeze. The streets were crowded with men and women, laughing and talking in happy voices. Doris and Douglas walked past fruit stalls, postcard shops and all kinds of refreshment stands. The music pulled them along, promising even more excitement.

"That's where the music is coming from," Doris said, pointing at a large building at the end of the street. On the ground floor there was a roller skating rink, and from above the music jitterbugged out into the night.

Dancers moved around the upper level, which was lit like a carnival.

"Let's go in," Douglas said as they neared the skaters.

"We can't," Doris pointed out. "No money."

"What if Father's in there?"

"Let's look other places first."

"I guess you're right," Doug said. They turned up another street, leaving the music and laughter behind.

"Where do you think we should look?" Doris asked. The street was getting darker, the houses farther apart. The hollow noise of loudspeakers became fainter and fainter.

"Look!" Douglas cried. He pointed at a sign hanging from an iron railing. "It's Missus Nettie's sister."

"Palmist," Doris read. "Madame Pierrot." Douglas crept to the window. He peeked inside and waved Doris forward.

Doris glanced up and down the street, then crawled to where Douglas was hiding in the bushes. A well-dressed woman was sitting at a table, her back to the window. Facing her was a large Negro woman. The palmist! As she cut some cards, the light flashed brightly on her rings and earrings. She wore a purple turban and a crimson dress. Her voice was low and melodious and carried through the window into the darkness.

"Your troubles are almost over," she said. The other woman leaned forward, murmuring.

"Oh, yes! I see it! You have a journey in your future."

A tinkling laugh. The wrought iron gate clanged. A group of three people climbed the steps and milled about on the wooden porch.

"You knock, Sally," said one, laughing.

"I'll do it," said a man's voice. He knocked loudly, causing the women to giggle.

Douglas and Doris ducked down into the shrubbery under the window. Inside, a chair scraped against wooden boards as Madame Pierrot left the room. The other lady rose and began to pace, her shadow passing back and forth across the lawn.

The front door opened, spilling light onto the front walk.

"You're early!" exclaimed Madame Pierrot.

"Do you mind if we wait?" the man asked.

The group scuffled into the hall and the door closed, shutting off the light.

Madame Pierrot's voice drew closer as she reentered the room where the lady waited to hear her future.

The pacing shadow returned to its seat. The reading continued.

"You will take a ship to England, where you will be married."

Doris rose up again, the voices attracting her like an insect to a porch light.

"Will I be happy?" asked the tinkling voice.

"Happiness is not an event," came the reply. "It is a state of mind. It is not something I can predict."

The newcomers grew rowdy, and the reading drew to a close.

"Let's go," Doris said, pulling Douglas by the arm. "There's nothing here."

"Let's get her to tell us our future," Douglas said.

"Are you crazy?" Doris hissed. "That takes money."

"Everything takes money," muttered Douglas. "Hey!" he said, brushing her hand away. "Maybe she wants to send a message to her sister."

"Let's go, Douglas," Doris said, heading to the street. "We've got to find Father."

Doris hadn't eaten since breakfast, and her stomach was an empty hole, her knees wobbly. The lights of town twinkled in the distance, and Doris thought of all the food vendors they had passed on their way up the street.

"Let's go back home," she said.

"Uh," Douglas stammered as he caught up with her.

"What?" she asked.

"I forgot to tell you. We can't get back until tomorrow."

"Tomorrow! What will Mother think?"

"I don't care!" Douglas stopped dead in the middle of the road. "She's planning on moving us to Alberta. Maybe I won't ever go back. Maybe I'll just take off and ride the rails, like Father." His voice caught when he said "Father."

"You wouldn't dare!" Doris imagined Mother's horrified face when she discovered her children were missing. She remembered Billy McKenzie's mother, and her throat tightened.

"Yeah, well I'm not moving to Alberta."

Douglas started walking again, scuffing up dirt as he went. Doris ran after him. "You think that Madame Pierrot is cozening that lady?" asked Doris, trying out her new word.

"You and your dumb words!" Douglas snorted.

"Well it's better than running around with rum-runners."

"You can't eat words," Douglas said.

"Oh, yes, you can," said a voice coming from behind, chuckling. "Leastways, that's what my wife expects me to do."

Doris and Douglas wheeled around. A large Negro man was standing three feet behind them.

"What are you two bickering about?" he asked.

"Who are you?" Douglas said.

"I was about to ask you the same thing," he said in a low voice. "And I figure I've got a right to know, since you two were just now peeking in my window."

Douglas yelled, "Run!" He bolted for the trees.

The man's hand closed around Doris' arm. "You forget something, young man?" he called. He hoisted Doris up and tucked her under his arm like a loaf of bread. Doris' feet churned in the air behind her.

"Let me go!"

The man laughed deep in his chest. "Easy now, Missy. Nobody's going to hurt you. But my wife saw you two rapscallions peeking in her window and she sent me along to bring you in for questioning." He laughed again and turned back toward the palmist's house, Doris still under his arm.

"Douglas!" Doris yelled over her shoulder.

"I imagine he'll be right along, young miss. Not to worry." The man's voice was deep and rumbly, like distant thunder.

He carted Doris up the wooden steps and into the front hallway. Lamps were lit on a hall table, covered by shades made from hundreds of tiny bits of colored glass that formed the pattern of an exotic-looking flower. The room smelled sweet, and Doris saw a vase of sweet peas on a sideboard in a sitting room. A jewel-colored carpet covered the floor, swirling with deep reds and sapphires like something out of the *Arabian Nights.*

The man plunked Doris down on a silk-covered chair. "You'd best not try and run away, little miss. I'd hate to have to chase after you again."

Doris looked around for a means of escape. The man shut the front door and, keeping one eye on Doris, opened the door to the room where Doris had seen the palmist reading the fortune of the well-dressed lady.

"Caught the young miss, Elmira," he said, smiling a wide smile.

Madame Pierrot appeared in the doorway. Up close, she was even grander and wider and stronger than she had seemed through the window.

She beckoned to Doris to come forward, then

stood aside and pointed at the chair where the woman with the tinkling laugh had had her fortune told.

Doris' trembling knees would barely support her weight. The giant man nudged her with the palm of his hand. "Go on," he said.

"I, I, I'm sorry we spied on you," Doris stammered.

"Land sakes, child, is that what you think this is all about? Louis, what on earth did you tell this girl?" Madame Pierrot looked accusingly at her husband.

"Didn't tell her a thing. Thought she and that boy might learn a lesson or two about what happens to Peeping Toms."

Madame Pierrot shook her head. "No wonder the child's so scared she can barely walk. Come here, girl."

Doris forced herself to stop trembling. She took a deep breath and put one foot forward. Madame Pierrot held out her hand.

"Lordy, Lordy, I won't bite."

Doris inched forward until she was at the door of the inner sanctum. The man's chuckling gave way to full-out belly laughing. Madame Pierrot shot him an annoyed look, pulled Doris into the room and shut the door.

"Sit down, child," said Madame Pierrot, gesturing at the chair opposite hers at the table.

Doris sat on the edge of the seat. The room smelled like some exotic incense. There was a crystal ball on the sideboard and a teapot with a selection of cups on the table in front of her. The walls were papered with photographs of famous people, and with even the slightest breeze the wind chimes that hung in the window tinkled like the lady's laughter.

Madame Pierrot grinned as she sat down. "You know why I asked Louis to bring you here?"

Doris gulped and shook her head. The wind chimes sent a gentle music throughout the room.

"I saw you and that boy." She paused and cocked an eyebrow. "Your brother, I presume?"

"Yes, ma'am."

"Well, I saw you two peeking in my window. Oh, don't look so worried." She deftly shuffled the cards and started laying them out in front of her. "It happens all the time. Children come and spy on me for lots of reason. Curiosity." She tapped one of the cards and wrinkled her forehead. "Dares." She rearranged two cards. Then she looked up, riveting Doris with her eyes. "But with you, I sensed something else."

Doris squirmed in her seat.

"I sensed," said Madame Pierrot, "a burning question. I saw something when I looked at you, and it interfered with my reading for Miss Woods."

She stared hard at Doris, her brown eyes melting into dark pools.

Was she being hypnotized? Doris blinked rapidly and looked longingly at the closed door.

"I felt I needed to read your cards," Madame Pierrot said. She scooped the cards back into a pile and pushed it across the table to Doris. "Cut," she commanded.

Doris split the deck in two. Madame Pierrot dealt the cards.

She glanced at Doris. "So where do you come from, child?"

The story of the rumrunning boat and the ferry crossing spilled out of Doris before she knew what she was saying. She gulped. Did this woman have a secret power over her?

"Hmmm," Madame Pierrot said as she studied Doris' face. "That's most informative." She glanced down at her cards.

"What do you see?" asked Doris.

"I see a long journey. To a new place. A new beginning."

Doris shook her head. That's what she'd told Miss Woods.

"And I see someone crying. A woman."

Doris thought of her mother coming back from Leamington to discover her children missing. She crossed her arms over her chest.

"I see a man. It is a shadowy image, not clear. Like an outline that is not filled in."

"Where is this man?" Doris asked in a hoarse voice.

"You haven't seen this man for a long time." Madame Pierrot's voice became low and trance-like. "He is not well."

A flash of movement caught Doris' eye. She glanced at the window. Madame Pierrot's eyes were closed as if she were watching a movie screen inside her head. Douglas' white face appeared in the glass. Doris gasped. Madame Pierrot's eyes flew open.

"He is nearby."

The bushes crashed and scratched against the wooden house.

"Leave me alone" came Douglas' frantic yell.

"Got him!" said Louis, hoisting Douglas up by his collar.

Madame Pierrot nodded, and the bushes fell silent. The next thing Doris heard was Douglas' voice in the vestibule. Then he was in the doorway, leaves stuck to his hair.

"You all right, Doris?" he said, clenching his fists

as if he was about to hit the giant man who still had a grip on his collar.

"Yes," Doris said, rising from her seat.

"Wait!" Madame Pierrot murmured. Her eyes were closed again, her hand raised in an attempt to quiet Douglas.

The room fell silent.

"He needs your help."

"Who?" Doris managed to stammer.

"Your father."

Chapter 10

"Father?" repeated Douglas. The man let go of his collar, and Douglas stumbled into the room.

Madame Pierrot took Doris' hand and turned it over. She studied it like a road map, tracing the lines with the tip of her finger.

"What is your name, Missy?" Madame Pierrot asked.

"Doris Stanley."

Madame Pierrot and Louis exchanged glances over Doris' head.

"What do you need to know her name for?" demanded Douglas.

"Just calm down, son," said Louis. "We don't mean you any harm."

"Stanley?" Madame Pierrot looked thoughtful. "Where do you come from, child?"

"Windsor," answered Doris.

"You know a Fred Stanley?" Madame Pierrot said. She dropped Doris' hand and pushed her cards into a loose pile.

"That's my father's name," Douglas said.

Madame Pierrot stood and put her hand on Douglas' shoulder. A chill crept down Doris' spine. How could anyone tell the future? It was impossible.

"How did you two end up here?"

"We're spending the summer on Point Pelee. Pete Long told us he'd seen a man who looked like our father."

"You haven't seen him for quite a while." It was not a question.

"Not for two years."

Madame Pierrot nodded. "Time can make a big difference in a man. You'll have to understand."

"Understand what?" Douglas cried. His voice cracked. It hadn't done that for months.

"Louis," said Madame Pierrot. "Show the children where their father is."

"You sure?" he asked.

She nodded. "They have to know."

Doris didn't like the way Madame Pierrot was staring at her. Her eyes were sad.

"Come on, then." Louis started toward the door, Douglas at his heels.

Doris hesitated. Madame Pierrot nodded. "Go ahead, child. You have the courage."

Louis led them down the back steps of the house, through the backyard and into an overgrown lane. Dogs barked along the route, hurling themselves against wooden fences. A light came on in the house at the corner and a man yelled, "Quiet, Rufus!" A shoe spiraled out an open bedroom window, and the dog yelped.

"This way," said Louis, beckoning for them to follow.

The sound of the saxophones and drums drowned out the insect chorus as they got closer to the wharf.

"You children wait here," Louis said as he slipped inside a shack just outside the rifle range.

Doris' stomach pitched and tossed. Douglas ran his nails up and down his arm, leaving gouges in his skin.

"This is it, Doris," he said. His eyes glistened. "Do you really think it's him?"

The prickling on the back of her neck told her it had to be. She closed her eyes and commanded herself to stay calm. She heard voices: Louis and someone else, arguing. She would know that voice anywhere. Douglas stopped scratching his arm and froze. They looked at each other.

They knew.

"You can go in now." Louis held open the rickety door.

Douglas went first. He moved as if in slow motion. Time stood still. Doris' breathing was shallower than a well in a drought. She followed.

A dim light inside the shack came from a kerosene lamp on top of an old crate. A man sat in an awkward fashion, propped against a pile of dirty clothes. His face was streaked with dirt. His eyes flicked back and forth from one child to the other.

"Father?" Doris asked. This ragged bundle of clothes couldn't be her father. It was impossible. She called up her memories. Father, laughing at the antics of her kitten, his face tanned and alive. The kitten dangling with its baby claws from the leg of his pants as he walked across the kitchen floor.

His leg. She knew what the difference was. It wasn't just the haunted look in his eyes or the dirty matted hair. The man tried to hoist himself to his feet, reaching for a makeshift crutch as he did so.

The man only had one leg.

"Father?" echoed Douglas, staring at the folded pant leg and the man's unsteady hopping as he moved toward them across the uneven floor.

"Doris. Douglas." The man's eyes held a desperate appeal.

"Well, now. I guess you all want to be alone." Louis backed away as quietly as a cat stalking a bird, the door shutting silently behind him.

The man stumbled; the crutch flew out from under his arm.

Without thinking, Doris rushed to his side. His arm closed over her shoulder. He buried his face in her hair. Doris wrapped her other arm around his waist, feeling the bones of his ribs.

He smelled of wood smoke and earth. He smelled of sickness and disappointment. He smelled of hundreds of days without food. He smelled of stale whiskey. He smelled like a different person.

"It's so good to see you," he said.

Doris eased him onto a bale of straw.

Douglas stood rooted to the spot.

"Son?"

Douglas shook his head. His eyes filled with tears. Doris knew he was trying his darndest not to cry. But sometimes crying was all there was to do.

"Douglas?" she said.

Doug broke. His tears spilled over his eyes. He took a step forward. Then another. Then they were all holding on together.

Chapter 11

"I got hurt trying to jump a freight train outside Winnipeg."

Douglas and Doris sat on the floor, staring up into the eyes of the stranger who was their father.

"They took me to a doctor, and he cut it off."

Doris winced.

"That was last January," Father said. "After it healed, I couldn't ride the rails anymore. I couldn't get work." He stroked his beard. "I couldn't get home. And I didn't think your mother needed to put up with a cripple. I thought I'd best stay away."

"Why didn't you write?"

"I wanted to. I thought I would. But I knew your mother would tell me to come back, that she would take care of me. Out of duty. I thought it best to stay silent."

Doris shook her head.

Douglas chewed on a piece of straw. "You have to come home now."

"How's your mother?" Father asked.

"She's written her father. He's traveled to Leamington to see her. She says we have to go live with him."

A shadow crossed Father's face, highlighting the hollows in his cheeks.

"That must have been difficult for her to do."

"She says we have no choice."

"Maybe she's right."

Doris looked into her father's face. It was not going to be all right. He was not going to make things just the way they were.

"How did you know I was here?" asked Father.

Douglas told him how Pete Long had spotted him.

"How did you get here?" Doris said.

"Got on one last train with the help of a few friends. Brought me as far as Sandusky. One of the fellows told me to come here, that his cousin would give me a place to stay in return for loading the guns at the rifle range."

"You've got to come home, Father."

He shook his head. "I'm no use to your mother."

"What about us?" Douglas demanded.

Father dropped his eyes. "I'm no good to anyone."

Douglas turned and ran. He disappeared into town, toward the harbor and the bright lights of the entertainment booths. Father tried to stand, but couldn't hop more than a few feet. "You see?" he yelled.

Doris looked at the way Douglas had gone. Then she looked at Father.

"Go," he said. "Just go." He sank to the floor and buried his face in his hands.

Doris had never seen Father cry before. She didn't know what to say. Father waved her away with his hand.

She backed out into the night.

Douglas was sitting on the end of the pier, shooting stones into the rippling water.

"You've got to get over that temper, Douglas," she said.

"He's right," Doug muttered. "He's no good to anyone."

"We've got to understand," Doris said.

"Understand that he was never coming back? Well, I got that part understood just fine."

"No. We've got to know he wants to. Like those butterflies. Like how they always fly around the glacier. Then they get on track. We got to get Father around that glacier, Doug. We got to do it."

Doug continued to pitch stones into the water, where they sank in ripples of light into the dark lake.

"I'm going to go get him," she said. "I'm bringing him back. He just has to know we want him."

Douglas sat, his back rigid.

Doris turned and went along the dock. Behind her, stones continued to fall.

Plunk. Plunk. Plunk.

"I never finished telling you your future," said a voice from the dark.

Doris jumped. Madame Pierrot was standing at the corner.

Piano music danced into the night from an open window.

"What are you doing here?" Doris asked.

"Like I said. I had unfinished business."

Madame Pierrot fell into step beside Doris. They walked up the hill. Doris longed to look back, but she forced herself not to. Douglas was going to have to make up his own mind. Doris had made up hers.

"You have a great future ahead of you," said Madame Pierrot as they neared the turnoff to her house. She touched Doris on the arm. "I have a very strong sense of this. You know that the wind fans a strong flame," she said. "It puts a small flame out."

She smiled. "I don't think that your fire will go out that easily." She put an envelope into Doris' hand. "I owe you this."

"What is it?"

"It's twenty dollars."

Twenty dollars! "What for?"

"For delivering the message."

"What message?" Doris was confused.

"The message that the *Yankee Clipper* was searched by the Coast Guard."

Doris gulped. She stared at Madame Pierrot's deep eyes. Was she a bootlegger?

"Never you mind, child," Madame Pierrot said as if reading her mind. "Just remember what I said." She patted Doris' head. "And by the way, those words you learn every day will prove mighty handy. It's your destiny."

Then she was gone.

Chapter 12

The ferry sliced through the water as gulls soared overhead.

Douglas ran from the stern. He plunked himself down beside Doris. "It's much nicer not hiding in the closet," he said.

Doris nodded. She didn't even feel as seasick, up on deck.

Beside her, Father stretched his good leg out in front of him. Madame Pierrot had given him some new clothes and a place to wash. He looked like a faded, smaller version of the father Doris remembered.

"Almost there," he said. His voice trembled.

Madame Pierrot had called Ida Carter at the Point Pelee store and let Doris tell her that she and Douglas were safe. Mrs. Carter had said she'd take a message to Mother so she wouldn't worry. Doris hadn't told her about Father.

She put her hand in Father's. He smiled and squeezed her fingers.

Douglas scowled at the seagulls.

After a brief stop at Pelee Island, they continued to Leamington. As the dock got closer and closer, Doris' stomach got jumpier and jumpier.

Douglas shaded his eyes with his hand and peered into the distance.

"I see her!"

Doris pulled her hand from Father's and stood up. People lined the dock, too fuzzy to make out.

"No you don't!" Doris said, poking Douglas in the ribs.

"I do so. Look!"

Doris squinted at where he was pointing. She could just make out the tall, gangly form of Mr. Mullins. She dropped her eyes. Doug was right! Mother stood beside him. And beside Mother was another man she didn't recognize.

"Who's that?" asked Douglas, as if reading her mind.

Father had come up behind them. "That's your grandfather," he said.

Doris stared. This was the evil man who was going to take them to Calgary? The one who caused

Mother and Father to fight? Her breath caught in her throat.

Mother saw them and started to wave. Then she saw the tall man behind them, and her arm froze.

The ferry steamed in to the dock, and the group on shore disappeared in the crowds of passengers.

"Hang onto me, Father," Doris said as they crossed the slippery deck.

"And me," said Douglas, holding out his arm.

Father gripped their arms.

"Hello, Fred," Mother said when the three stepped onto the dock. Father's hand trembled on Doris' shoulder.

A short, stout man with wire-rimmed spectacles held out his hand. "Fred," he said. The light glinted off his glasses.

Father held out his hand. "Ira," he said.

The man nodded stiffly. He looked at Doris and Douglas.

"Children, meet your grandfather," Mother said.

He was well dressed in freshly pressed clothes and carried a walking stick. His white hair was slicked back, and he had three chins.

"Hello, young man, young lady."

It sure was hard to believe that this was Mother's father. She didn't look a bit like him.

Doris gave him a good hard look. He was stern-faced, but there was something about him that she liked. Maybe it was the smile lines around the corners of his eyes. Or the softening of his mouth when he looked at Mother.

Mr. Mullins beckoned to Doris and Douglas. "Let's give these folks some privacy."

Doris stared over her shoulder as Mr. Mullins led her away. Mother and Father were looking at each other as if they didn't know whether to laugh or cry.

Grandfather listened as Father spoke. Mother reached out a tender hand to touch Father's face.

Doris started skipping.

Optimism, she thought. Maybe everything was going to be just as it was before Father left after all.

She smiled.

chapter 13

"I wonder what Calgary will be like," Douglas said as he put the last of his clothes into his old suitcase. Outside the window a rooster crowed.

"It won't be Windsor," Doris said.

"Hey," Douglas told her, giving her a push. "Cheer up."

"I never thought it would work out this way," Doris said. "I sure will miss our old street."

"Yeah," said Douglas as he sat beside her, sinking into the mattress. "I'll sure miss Killer and Mr. Barzelli." He grinned.

"And Ford Beach," Doris said, ignoring him.

"And Johnnie Mullins," Douglas teased.

"And Mavis Miller," Doris teased back.

Douglas blushed.

"Stop grousing," he said. He put on the new shirt Grandfather had bought him.

"You two ready?" called Mother from downstairs.

"Almost," Douglas yelled.

Doris' eyes prickled and her nose filled.

"Hey, Pipsqueak," said Douglas. "Don't cry."

"Do you really think Father will like working at Grandfather's insurance company?"

"I don't know," he said. "He's going to try."

"Mother said we'll all be living in the same house."

"I know."

"I don't think I'll like that." Doris thought of reading the funny papers on the verandah of their old house in Windsor. Of the musty smell of the street after a rain. Of walking through the vacant lots and picking cherries off the trees that grew wild in the lanes. She thought of Mrs. Gordon's store and the smells of Christmas. Of the barrels full of nuts, the peppermint candies, the giant suckers. She could hear the sounds of the radio, the announcers calling the game from Navin field in Detroit. The Vernor's Ginger Ale sign smiling at her from the other side of the river. She sniffed.

Douglas stood up and crossed over to the other side of the room.

"It's not like you to feel sorry for yourself, Doris Stanley," he said.

Doris swiped the back of her hand under her nose. Douglas didn't understand! No one did. This was not the way she had planned for things to work out.

"So I better give you this to cheer you up." Douglas handed her a brown-paper-wrapped parcel.

Doris fingered the string. "What's this?" Douglas had never given her a present before.

"Better open it and find out, Pipsqueak," he said.

Doris pulled off the wrapper. It was a notebook. An empty, blue-lined notebook.

She looked up.

"Don't you know what it's for?" Douglas asked.

"No."

"So you can write it all down, Doris. All the things you're going to miss. All those blasted words you keep learning. So you can put it there and make it into a story."

Doris blinked. A tear dropped on the back of her hand and she wiped it on her leg. It wouldn't do to smear the perfect blue lines of her new notebook. No sir.

Madame Pierrot's words danced in her head. "Those words are your destiny."

"Thanks, Douglas," Doris said, sniffing.

"Just write it all down."

"Time to go!" Father yelled.

"Come on," said Douglas.

"Be right there," Doris said. Douglas went out the door, grabbing his suitcase on the way.

Doris opened her notebook and smoothed the first page back. She wet the end of a fat Ticonderoga pencil that she had in her pack.

The Reunion, she wrote in big capital letters. She thought a minute, then added, *A True Story by Doris Stanley.*

"Doris!" called Grandfather.

Doris shut the book, took one last look around and ran downstairs.

She couldn't wait to see what would happen next.

Background Notes

Summer on the Run took shape in my mind when I attended a "Spirit Walk" that was enacted by the park staff on Point Pelee one fall evening two years ago. During the spirit walk, the park interpreters dramatized different eras in the Point's history, and I was fascinated by the scene showing two children escaping from the park ranger while illegally camping during the 1930s. Families from both Windsor and Detroit would camp on the Point during the Great Depression to save money on rent during the summer months.

The Windsor/Detroit border was also a scene of great rumrunning activity during the 1920s and early 30s. This was a time called Prohibition, and the selling and drinking of alcohol was illegal. Fortunes were made and lost during this period, and some estimate that as much as four-fifths of all the liquor smuggled to the United States went across the Detroit River. Al Capone, the legendary gangster, was spotted all around Windsor and Detroit in those days, and although rumrunning had slowed by the time of the Great Depression, it was still going on in 1931.

It was a time when children had a great deal more freedom than they do today. There were no TVs, computers, video games or DVD players. And although times were harsh, those I've talked to have clear and positive memories of these years as an exciting time to grow up. They may have had very little in the way of material possessions, but the fun and adventures they created from nothing more than made up for it.

Acknowledgments

I would like to sincerely thank a number of people for their help in pulling together the background information for *Summer on the Run*. I would first like to thank Sarah Rupert, Senior Park Interpreter and Education Coordinator at Point Pelee, for her guidance in recreating the locations of the orchard, the fishery and the squatters' campsites on Point Pelee in 1931. I would also like to thank Ron Tiessen of Pelee Island for his suggestions, input and recommendations about reading material that depicted island life in this period. And finally, I would especially like to thank the late Al Roach and his wife, Joyce, for kindly spending an afternoon with me, reminiscing about being a Depression-era boy growing up in the Border City.

The idea for *Summer on the Run* came to **Nancy Belgue** while she was on a "spirit walk" on Point Pelee. The park staff acted out skits from different points in the park's history, including one from the thirties in which displaced families squatted on the point to save money on rent. And, she says, she has always been fascinated by the dynamics between bothers and sisters. Nancy is also the author of *The Scream of the Hawk* (Orca, 2003), a Silver Birch nominee for 2005.